DATE DUE

GAYLORD   PRINTED IN U.S.A.

WORMWOOD,
NEVADA

ALSO BY DAVID OPPEGAARD

The Suicide Collectors

David
Oppegaard

WORMWOOD, NEVADA

St. Martin's Press
New York

Excerpts from *Rocks from Space*, by O. Richard Norton, © 1998, reprinted with permission by Mountain Press Publishing Company.

www.stmartins.com

Design by Susan Walsh

ISBN 978-0-312-38111-0

First Edition: December 2009

10 9 8 7 6 5 4 3 2 1

For Sarah Morse

Evolutionary biologists and their cousins the paleontologists know that life on this planet has not been a smooth progression of uninterrupted evolution of species. There have been numerous global mass extinctions throughout the 600 million years of multicellular life on this planet.

—O. Richard Norton, Rocks from Space

BOOK I

THE ARRIVAL

They left the city. They passed beyond the ripening cornfields and lush green plains and entered the desert. Anna moaned in her sleep as Tyler drove, pushing the car past eighty as he absorbed Nevada's landscape. He hadn't seen another car for thirty, forty minutes. Early June, and the countryside was nothing but a pale sea of sagebrush beneath an unbelievably bright sun. No mule deer, no cottontails, no frolicking antelope. The nature textbooks made it seem like the Great Basin Desert was a wonderland of biological diversity, with this hidden natural world beneath it, but that was like saying outer space was packed with matter because it contained microscopic specks of stardust. Right now, as far as Tyler Mayfield could see, he and his wife might have been the last two living creatures on earth.

They crested a hill. Red sunlight flared in the rearview mirror, filling the entire car with light. Half blinded, Tyler adjusted the mirror until it angled down. Dark, almond-shaped eyes stared back at him, cold and unblinking. Tyler swore and slammed on the brakes, twisting the steering wheel hard left. The Volvo spun around three times, almost flipping, before it squealed to a shuddering halt in the middle of the highway. Tyler unbuckled his seatbelt and scrambled around.

The backseat was empty.

"What the hell, Tyler?"

Anna was awake now, her blue eyes open and darting, her long, tan legs jammed into the floor. Even when she was freaked out, Tyler had to admit she still had that beauty queen glow.

"I thought I saw something."

"Where?"

"In the backseat. I thought something was back there."

Ann exhaled. "Fuck, Tyler."

"I'm sorry."

"Whatever. Just keep driving. We can't stop in the middle of the highway."

Tyler slapped his cheeks and gripped the steering wheel at ten and two o'clock. He took his foot off the brake and accelerated until they regained speed. He shivered, remembering the dark eyes, and slapped his cheek again. Anna dug into her purse, pulled out a tube of lip gloss, and opened her visor's. "You're going crazy from all the driving, Ty. You need to chill." Anna folded up the visor. "Hey. You see that blob up ahead?"

Tyler blinked, trying to focus. "I think so. Against those mountains?"

"Yeah. I bet it's a town."

"Sure it is. Civilization."

They drove another minute and turned off the highway onto a paved county road. After all the miles of red sand and malformed scrub, the town of Wormwood wavered in front of them. Tyler drove slowly, trying to take all the disappointment in.

Wormwood sat beneath a north-south mountain chain, two miles back from the highway. They passed a boxy, windowless casino on the edge of town. The road hooked right and revealed two gas stations, a U-Haul office, and several trailer homes before officially becoming Main Street. Here, aluminum-sided bungalows crowded out the trailer homes. Sun-scorched lawns displayed faded patio furniture, blown fireworks, and slick plastic wading pools slowly melting in the heat. Downtown was a grocery store, a Mexican restaurant, a diner, a bar, and an old man sitting in front of the post office, fanning himself with a large-print *TV Guide*. They turned left off Main Street, went five blocks, and turned right onto a street that ended in a gray, two-story house surrounded by a high picket fence.

Tyler turned the car off and listened to his wife's steady breathing. The Volvo's hot engine ticked, and in a moment the cooling fan whirred on. Tyler unbuckled his seatbelt. He rubbed his temples and the miles of interstate blurred through his mind, meshing into one flat expanse of rolling land and blue sky, with some rounded mountains in the far distance. Wormwood's closest neighboring town, Silverton, was sixty-seven miles behind them.

A woman in mirrored brown sunglasses emerged from the gray house and stood on her front steps, smoking a cigarette as she watched the car. Her hair was silver and short, but Tyler still recognized the woman from the faded pictures he'd been shown. He stepped out of the car. "Aunt Bernice?"

The woman came to the fence's gate. She was sixty and had a thick, sturdy frame much like his mother's.

"Call me Bernie. You Tyler?"

"Yes, ma'am."

"Hell's bells. Your mother was right. You could be Uncle Frank, thirty years ago. It's good to finally meet you, Ty. That your wife?"

Tyler looked over his shoulder. Anna was standing behind him, shading her face with a magazine.

"Sure is. Anna, meet my aunt, Bernie Turner."

"Hello, Bernie."

"Howdy. Aren't you a pretty little thing."

"Thank you," Anna said. "I like your sunglasses."

Bernie smiled and unlatched the gate. "Why don't you two come inside? I'll whip up some hard lemonade and you can cool off."

Tyler bit his lip as his wife glanced down the street. He knew what she was thinking, but what could he do about it? He wasn't God. He hadn't created central Nevada. The wind came up and rolled a tumbleweed toward them, as if on cue. "A drink sounds really good, actually," Anna said. "Thank you." Aunt Bernie held the gate and closed it behind them. She led them across a stony yard littered with potted cacti and dry, whitewashed birdbaths. "Folks," Bernie said, kicking a rock out of their path, "welcome to Wormwood."

Cold air enfolded Anna Mayfield as soon as she stepped in the house, causing her to halt inside the front hall and thank the sweet lord for air-conditioning. After two days of driving through Nebraska, Wyoming, Utah, and a chunk of Nevada in the summertime, any place cool and dark was fine with her. She could already feel her skin beginning to cool, her tank top peeling away from her back and stomach. Now maybe if she could just stand here quietly for a few minutes, not talking to anyone, she'd start to feel a little more human again. Get that smile back—

The door creaked open behind her. Heat rushed inside, raising the hall's temperature a good twenty degrees.

"What are you looking at?"

"Shut the door, Tyler."

He let the handle go and the door slammed shut. Anna went on into the living room. Tyler's aunt, who moved faster than you'd expect from an old high school lunch lady, had already crossed the room and stood watching them enter, her hands clasped in front of her. "Well, this is it, everyone. Casa de Turner."

Anna smiled. Here was the living room time forgot. Sunlight shone through the room's bay window and its gauzy white curtains, revealing an assortment of pea-green, seventies style furniture that was arranged in the traditional armchair-sofa-armchair formation around a long Formica coffee table. Yellow and lime gingham wallpaper. Dense white shag carpeting. Across the room a hulking thirty-five-inch TV sat on a brown stand, facing the furniture and as unavoidable as a black hole. On top of the TV was a framed photo of *Star Trek*'s Leonard Nemoy.

Tyler followed her into the living room and stood blinking. Anna took a second to examine her husband of six years as if he were part of the room, maybe a chaise longue, or a coatrack. They'd started dating in college, both of them English majors with no idea what they wanted to do for a living, and they'd gotten married right out of school. At six foot one, Tyler was a good three inches taller than Anna, a fact she had always appreciated since it allowed her to wear high heels when the situation called for it, and his skin was a creamy brown she envied. On the other hand, Tyler also had gangly arms, narrow shoulders, and squinted too much. He would have made a good assistant to a mad scientist.

Tyler picked up the photo on top of the TV. "Cool. Spock."

"Don't paw that," Bernie said. "It's autographed."

"Oh. Sorry."

Tyler set the picture down and stepped back. Bernie smiled.

"No mind. Let me go see about that lemonade."

Bernie disappeared as they sat down on the sofa. Anna rubbed her temples as her husband kicked off his sandals and wiggled his dirty toes. She should have made him put on socks at the last gas station. That would have cut down on the disgusting factor.

"Pretty sweet house, huh? I told you it'd be big enough for all three of us."

"Maybe we should go back, Ty."

"What? To Lincoln?"

"Sure. We could get temp jobs. It wouldn't be so bad."

Anna set a hand on her husband's bare knee. She let her fingers slip under his shorts and tease the fine hairs along his thigh. "You know, Ty, it was nice your aunt got you a job out here, but there's got to be better places to teach high school English. I mean, did you see the same town I saw out there?"

Tyler shifted away from her touch. "I like small towns."

"Since when?"

"Since forever. And she didn't get me the job. She just noticed an opening and told my mother about it. My résumé is what got me the job. Five years of substitute teaching should be good for something."

Anna slid farther down the couch. She was still trying to think of a stronger argument when the biggest dog she'd ever seen padded into the room and sniffed the air. Flat-out enormous, the dog was a cross between a golden retriever and a sheepdog, with shaggy, cream-colored fur that matched the carpeting. When the mutt trotted over to them, Anna's first instinct was to jump on the couch and ward him off with a pillow. Tyler smiled and scratched the dog behind his ears.

"Why hello, poochy. Do you live here, too?"

The dog grinned and showed his tongue.

"Ty, watch your hand."

"He's friendly," Tyler said, in that ridiculous cooing voice he always used with animals. "He just wants a good scratch."

Something clattered in the kitchen. The dog turned and rumbled off. The house smelled like dusty potpourri and, yeah, a little like dog. It reminded Anna of her grandmother's house, and that wasn't exactly the sort of place where you'd expect to find a young married couple, especially a former Miss Nebraska still capable of fitting into her high school blue jeans if she sucked it up a little.

"It's just for a year," Tyler said. "One year without rent and we'll have some money saved up."

"I think I smell denture cream."

"No, you don't."

"Well, I smell something. Something funky."

Tyler leaned into her and sniffed her hair. She could feel his hot breath on her neck and couldn't decide whether she was annoyed or turned on. It was always so damn close with him.

"You smell good."

"That's from the corn chips, Tyler. What you're smelling is nasty corn chip perfume."

Tyler took a deeper whiff and sighed. Anna pushed him

away and ran a hand through her greasy, road-trip hair. She felt disgusting. She could almost feel all the sugar and saturated fats from the last two days clogging her pores and settling on her hips. She'd need to get more facial cleanser somewhere. Did they even carry facial cleanser in Wormwood? Or how about makeup in general? Maybe the women around these parts settled for lard mixed with food coloring.

Bernie returned to the living room with three clinking glasses of hard lemonade, the dog at her heels. She set the glasses on the coffee table in a patch of sunlight and the drinks glowed yellow. Tyler took his glass with both hands and held it against his face. Bernie sat down in a recliner and kicked up the footrest. The dog turned around three times, yawned, and sank beside Bernie's recliner in a curled mound.

"You meet Roscoe?"

Anna and Tyler nodded as they drank their hard lemonade.

"I found him when he was just a pup. He was sniffing around the Dumpsters behind the high school, looking for scraps. Don't even know what kind of dog he is, really. Saint Bernard, maybe."

Anna felt her stomach warm.

"I'm sorry, I forgot to ask if you two even drink alcohol. I like to mix my lemonade with vodka."

Anna swallowed the lemonade. "Oh yeah, Bernie, we drink. We definitely drink."

"That's good," Bernie said. "I figure drinking's the most popular pastime in Wormwood. Everyone around here likes to throw back a few."

Anna smacked her lips. "Why not, right? I'm sure people around here aren't too busy going to the opera."

"No. I don't know too many opera fans from town. Do you folks like opera?"

"Hell no," Tyler said. "Who likes opera?"

"Opera fans," Anna said. "The cultured elite."

Bernie drained her glass. "You know what I like?" she said, smiling as she reclined in her chair. "Science fiction."

Anna frowned. "Science fiction?"

"Like *Star Trek*. You ever watch reruns of *Star Trek*?"

"Sure," Tyler said. "Sometimes."

"Everybody thinks Captain Kirk is such a sexy beefcake, but I like Spock. He's always so calm and thoughtful. Even when the ship's going to hell around him and aliens are attacking, he stays cool. I like that. I work in the school cafeteria, you know. You think we can get all flustered when we have three hundred mouths to feed? No way in hell. The little monsters would eat us alive and spit out the bones."

Bernie threw her head back and laughed. Anna finished her drink and set it on the table. The vodka was making her sleepy.

"Actually, I'm more of a *Star Wars* fan."

"*Star Wars?* No, thank you. There's your opera for you, right there. Your soap opera in space." Bernie stubbed out her cigarette and stood up. "You two look ready to slump over. Let me show you the guest room. We're partial to afternoon naps around here."

THREE

A lamp crashed. Anna opened one eye. Tyler had gotten out of bed and tripped over the lamp cord as he unpacked his suitcase. The man was like Helen Keller in a china shop. "Sorry, sorry," he whispered, setting the lamp upright. Anna closed her eye. She felt like she was still in the car, speeding down the highway at eighty miles an hour. Maybe this was all one bad car dream. Maybe they hadn't even arrived in Wormwood yet, or perhaps Wormwood wasn't really their destination. Maybe she'd wake up in San Francisco, covered in Ghirardelli chocolate and gay men.

"Anna."

Oh god. She hated the fake whisper. Tyler wasn't concerned about waking her up. He was trying to wake her up. Why even bother to whisper?

"Anna?"

Anna groaned and rolled over.

"I'm going to go for a walk. Scout around town."

"Fine."

"Do you need anything?"

"Sleep."

"Okay. I might be gone a few hours."

Anna pulled the blanket over her head. Tyler left the bedroom and tromped downstairs. Could you hear everything in this house? Anna pushed the blanket off and sat up in bed. The shades were drawn. She dipped a hand into her suitcase and pulled out a magazine. It was too dark to read the blocks of text, but she could make out the models well enough. Anna studied each picture carefully, weighing the pros and cons of each woman's figure and the way she presented herself to the camera. She held the magazine up to her nose and inhaled its gluey, perfumed scent. She could still remember every exciting minute of the Miss Nebraska circuit. Only eighteen, she'd juggled the demands of the pageant with the demands of her senior year at prep school. She'd been exhilarated by the challenge, the whole marathon quality of it all. Giving interviews, creating a winning platform, fund-raising, smashing through every local event. And the Miss Nebraska Scholarship Pageant itself, three dizzying nights in the Performing Arts Center of North Platte High School. She'd been grilled, scrutinized, and combed over as closely as an astronaut in training, smiling as she ran circles around the other contestants, dealing with the ingratiatingly kind girls and the downright bitchy ones with the same ease and natural grace. She'd performed and been judged in turn, and in the end she'd won that sash.

Life had been so much more clear-cut back then.

So much simpler.

Anna tossed the magazine onto the floor. She lay back and fell asleep, snoring lightly into her feather pillow.

The heat enveloped Tyler as he stepped outside. It was dusk now, but it wasn't getting any cooler. He was glad Anna had decided to stay at the house. It felt good to walk alone after the long road trip and the sluggish afternoon nap. The homes he passed were silent, their shades drawn, their rocky yards empty of children. The entire town might have been asleep, united in a deep love of siestas. It wasn't hard to imagine a series of quiet days ahead, each one slightly more muffled. No doubt children walked alone safely to school in Wormwood, and older folks still left their cars unlocked. If Nebraska was relatively quiet and unpopulated, Wormwood was one step away from thick-bearded, mountain hermit status.

Tyler turned off his aunt's street and headed south, toward downtown. Wormwood was laid out like a grid. Streets intersected at right angles. Nothing meandered or curved. A block before Main Street, Tyler stopped at a scraggly patch of shrubs and picnic tables that must have been the town park. He sat at the nearest table and watched the sun set behind the mountains. They'd come so far after only two days of driving. He thought about Cody and wondered how he'd manage to find him now.

Tyler had been twelve when his older brother, a happy,

laid-back sixteen-year-old who played guitar and varsity baseball, had driven to the Westroads Mall one Saturday afternoon to buy a video game and failed to return. The police were called. A missing persons report was filed. Tyler's parents had overturned the entire house looking for a short note, a journal entry, some piece of evidence as to why their son had disappeared. They found nothing but a stack of nudie magazines under his mattress and half a pack of Camel Lights in his underwear drawer. The police never found Cody's car, his wallet, or anything else he'd taken with him. It was as if Cody Mayfield had made a wrong turn on the way to the mall and entered a foggy Nebraskan Triangle, never to be heard from or seen again.

Tyler put his hands behind his head and leaned back, stretching his lower back. Something sizable loomed over his shoulder, breathing warm, wet air down his neck. He turned slowly and looked into the muzzle of a white horse. The horse snorted and pawed the ground. "Howdy," the horse's rider said. "Don't mind Sadie. She's as gentle as a lamb." The rider was a lean gray-eyed man around fifty years old. He wore blue jeans, black snakeskin boots, and a tan cowboy hat. He also wore a tan Nevada sheriff department's shirt, complete with a shoulder mic and a star on the left breast pocket. The rider also wore a revolver on his hip, buttoned into a rawhide holster.

Tyler rubbed his eyes and refocused. "You're Wormwood's sheriff?"

"Yes, sir. Name's Merritt Jackson."

"Tyler Mayfield. I'm Bernie Turner's nephew."

"Ah. The Nebraskan nephew. You'll be teaching our kids about books and such. Literature."

"I'll try my best."

"You read westerns?"

"I've read a few."

Merritt shifted in his saddle. "I'm a Zane Grey man myself. Read everything he's written."

"Reading is a great escape," Tyler said, eyeing the horse as it bared its yellow teeth. Merritt switched the horse's reins from his left to right hand and pulled them so Sadie swiveled north. He pushed his cowboy hat up on his forehead and peered across the park. The street lamps had snapped on and thick clouds of bugs already swarmed in orbit. The sky wasn't totally dark yet, but it was getting close. The park's shrubs and picnic tables had been relegated to outlines, inked in black.

"You've been followed, Mr. Mayfield. Something caught your scent and followed you to the park."

"What?"

"It's big, too. Hiding over there."

The sheriff nodded at a quivering clump of juniper bushes twenty feet away. Tyler swung his legs out from under the picnic table and stood up to get a better view. "Damn," Merritt said. "I hope it's not a bear."

"A bear?"

"Sometimes they come down from the mountains, looking for food. In the old days, they liked to feed on prospectors.

The mining company still has trouble with them on occasion."

"Really? You think that's a bear?"

"Guess we'll find out."

Merritt patted Sadie on the neck and whispered in her ear. He sat back in the saddle, slipped two fingers into his mouth, and whistled. A blurry white mass exploded out of the bushes and bolted across the park. Merritt chuckled as the mass bounded off toward Main Street.

"Just old Roscoe, fooling around. You leave Bernie's gate open?"

"I don't remember. Guess I must have."

Merritt rubbed his hands on his blue jeans. "Suppose we better fetch him back before the station gets called."

"Sure. I'd appreciate the help."

They started after the dog in a comfortable silence, their pace unhurried as Tyler walked alongside the horse. The air smelled like cooking hamburger and fried onions. Mariachi music drifted out to the street from an open garage. Tyler ran a hand across his forehead, wiping off the sweat. Stars poked through the night sky like white Lite-Brite pegs, reminding Tyler of the unassuming plains back home.

FOUR

Buried under blankets and pillows in her sagging guest bed, Anna Mayfield dreamt she was sixteen again and back at St. Mary's, flitting from room to room in the prep school's dorm hall. All the girls were excited. A group of boys was going to sneak in later and they'd have a party. Anna ran down the smooth marble hallways in her stockings, not caring whether the socks got dirty, not caring whether they all got caught. She felt wild. Freaking wild, and it felt great. She took out her ponytail, shook her hair loose, and ran to the nearest window. Trees swayed on the lush grass lawn. A willow tree slapped at the air, as if it could also sense the wildness of the night and wanted to unplant itself, to get up and have a look around. Anna pulled at the window, wanting to smell the night, but the ancient iron frame wouldn't open. Someone shouted,

> The boys are here
> The boys are here

and Anna ran to the group as it swirled on the front lawn. A boy came up and hugged her off the ground. He smelled good, like aftershave mixed with soap. He whispered something she couldn't hear. Light flashed in the distance, so bright she could see it through her eyelids. Lightning?

No.

A plume of white light, rising into the dark sky.

The boys and girls headed inside the dorm, still chatting happily in party mode. Anna stayed out on the lawn by herself. Another plume of white, and flakes of ash began to drop from the sky like dead moths.

Anna held out her hand. A gray flake landed in her palm and curled upon itself. Anna took a step back on the lawn as the word "nuclear" occurred to her. She took another step back and one of her socks slipped off into the dewy grass. She broke for the dorm hall's front door and burst inside, running toward the loud voices, toward the people, but as she ran the old windows rattled in their lead frames, and that might as well have been a death knell.

Anna shot up in bed, gasping. Her blankets lay piled at the foot of the bed, twisted around her ankles. The room was dark, and for a few seconds she didn't know where she was. White dots floated across her vision. She set her feet on the floor and the nightmare receded. She remembered the trip from Lincoln to central Nevada. Meeting Tyler's aunt, drinking hard lemonade, and taking a nap. This was their bedroom now. This dark room was hers.

The bed creaked as Anna reached over to the nightstand and turned on a lamp. The shaded glow made the room seem more real, almost normal. The pillows had been knocked to the floor. The bed sheets had tiny pink carnations on them, and Anna rubbed at one with her thumb. She heard footsteps run up the stairway and stop outside the bedroom. Knuckles rapped against the door and Bernie poked her face inside the room.

"You okay, Anna? I heard you screaming."

"I had a nightmare."

"Must have been a bad one."

Tremors passed through Anna's legs, causing her knees to knock against each other. "The damn dog got out again," Bernie said, leaning against the doorway. "I was about to get my shoes on and go search for him."

"I'm trembling."

"What you need is some fresh air to calm your nerves. Why don't you help me look for Roscoe? It's cooler out now."

Anna clutched her knees with her hands until her legs stayed still.

"Sure, Bernie. Let's go find your dog."

FIVE

They crossed Main Street. Tyler looked both ways, but except for a few tumbling plastic bags the street was empty. They headed south, toward the center of town. Sadie's hooves clattered on the sidewalk pavement. They passed a Salvation Army. Its windows were dark and its sign flipped to CLOSED. Merritt leaned over in his saddle and spit on the road. "I'm pretty sure that dog's at the Mexican restaurant. He likes to go there when he gets loose. The smell drives him crazy."

The Mexican restaurant was a squat, rectangular building set twenty yards back from the street behind a large, asphalt-covered parking lot. It looked like an old Kentucky Fried Chicken painted gray, with a billboard slapped on the roof above the entryway that read

TACO THUNDER

and had an enormous, flaming hard-shell taco above it. Roscoe was outside the building's entryway, scrabbling at one of the glass doors in an effort to storm the restaurant. A man stood on the other side of the door, pounding on the glass and shouting at the dog.

They crossed the parking lot. Tyler cupped his hands around his mouth and shouted for the dog, but Roscoe ignored him and kept attempting to scale the door. Merritt's saddle creaked as he pulled out a length of rope.

"He won't listen to reason, son. Let me bring him in."

Merritt tied a wide loop at the end of the rope and tossed it across the parking lot with a flick of his wrist. The lasso dropped around Roscoe's neck and Merritt pulled it tight. As he did all this, the sheriff's expression didn't change, as if roping crazed dogs was something he did on a daily basis.

The restaurant's owner stepped outside as the sheriff reined in the dog. He was a tall Mexican American with wide shoulders, brown eyes, and a stomach that spilled over his waist like a pouch filled with too much gravy. His dark hairline had long ago receded to the rear of his scalp, but he kept what hair remained plastered to his skull in a messy comb-over.

"Evening, Mr. Diaz."

Mr. Diaz nodded at the sheriff, but kept his eyes on the dog. "That bitch slammed right into my door this time. Do you see this slobber? Guess who gets to clean that up? I'll give you one guess."

"Sorry about that," Tyler said. "He got out somehow."

"Who the hell are you?"

"I'm Tyler Mayfield."

Tyler stepped forward and held out his hand. Mr. Diaz ignored the hand and returned his full attention to the dog, which strained against the sheriff's rope to the point of gagging. "You ever try balancing accounts with a monster slamming against your front door? It fucks with you." Mr. Diaz ran a hand over his head, replastering his hair. "I just want to get my work done in peace. It's Friday night. Don't you think I want to be home by now, sitting in my underwear and drinking beer in front of the TV? I pay my taxes. Is a little peace and quiet so goddamn much to ask?"

"Not at all."

"Then why don't you take that beast away before it chokes itself to death on my property? How about you do that?"

Merritt handed Tyler the dog's rope and tipped his hat. "That sounds fine by me, Charles. Say hello to Rosa for me."

They headed back down Main Street. Roscoe kept pulling at the rope and yanking Tyler off his feet, so Tyler went with Plan B, a jerky, staggering walk that involved digging his heels into the ground and keeping his weight back. He thought the sheriff would volunteer to take the rope, but Merritt seemed oblivious to his tribulation. The sheriff had dismounted and was leading Sadie by the reins, occasionally murmuring to the horse as they walked along. They headed north on Main Street, aimed in unspoken agreement toward a brightly lit bar on the other side of the street. They tied the animals to a hitching post outside the bar, in front of a watering trough. Sadie eyed Roscoe suspiciously as the animals lowered their necks and drank. Roscoe paid no attention to the horse, spilling as much water as he took in. Merritt and Tyler left the animals to their refueling and entered the noisy bar.

Tyler scanned the crowd as his eyes adjusted to the light. Since his brother's disappearance, he liked to play a mental game called Find Cody. The rules were simple: You had to keep an eye out for any guy who looked like Cody, remembering to adjust for aging, new clothes, new hairstyles, and the possibility of random outliers such as tattoos, piercings, or missing limbs. Tyler played Find Cody every time he was in public, especially in well-populated restaurants, grocery stores, and bars. Every time he sat down in a movie theater or auditorium, Tyler scanned the crowd, studying faces on the off chance he'd find his brother staring back at him. Cody could be anywhere, waiting to be found.

They sidled up to a freestanding bar in the center of the room and sat down. A pasty-faced man in a dress shirt and red tie sat on Tyler's right, staring into a tumbler of gin.

"Evening, Clyde."

"Evening, Sheriff."

Country music played on the bar's jukebox, but no one was dancing. Two pool tables, both in use, were set on the other side of the room. Black, faux-leather booths lined the wall behind Tyler and the wall to his left. Couples sat in the booths, fiddling with cardboard coasters and cell phones as they talked and drank their beer. Tyler realized he and Anna would soon be another couple sitting in the booths. They'd probably become regulars. They'd learn everyone's name, and on Friday nights they'd come to this smoky bar to listen to sad country music and get drunk.

Merritt ordered a pitcher of beer from a pretty brunette bartender. She poured the pitcher and set two frosted glasses in front of them. Merritt filled the two glasses himself.

"Who's your friend, Sheriff?"

"Tyler Mayfield. Just blew in from Nebraska."

"Well, how about that. Hi, Tyler. I'm Tracy."

Tyler nodded. "Nice to meet you. Having a good night?"

Tracy swiped at the bar with a rag and glanced at Clyde. "Better than some, I guess."

They drank their beer while Tracy went off to help customers at the other end of the bar. Merritt poured a second round, and they drank that, too. During the third round Tyler made the mistake of making eye contact with Clyde, who immediately began speaking with Ancient Mariner intensity.

"You know how it gets real quiet before a thunderstorm? The air pressure falls and the birds chirp a lot and the ground animals get uneasy and start snorting? This week it was like that around our house. My wife would enter a room without making any noise and get whatever and before I could say boo she was off in another room, like something had pinched her in the ass. What could I do about that? What's a guy say when anything he says is worse than saying nothing at all, and nothing at all is just making her angrier and angrier? It's not like I cheated on her, though I could have. You hang around this bar long enough and you know who's open for business. Even a guy like me gets some looks sometimes. But no, I never cheated on her, but I couldn't make her happy, either. She was a rock and a hard place all rolled into one."

Merritt Jackson shifted on his barstool. "Clyde, maybe your lady leaving was for the good. This could be a whole new life for you."

"She made the best peach cobbler. The best."

"Peach cobbler ain't everything. There's something to be said for peace and quiet. Hell, I'm not married, and I can get peach cobbler at the diner whenever I want for three bucks."

"It's not the same, Sheriff."

"Fair enough. But I'm sure twenty-five years of marriage wasn't all kisses and peach cobbler."

Clyde murmured into his drink. Merritt winked at Tyler and took a drink of his beer. "You know, Clyde, when I was younger, I wanted this one horse real bad. She was an Appaloosa, big as a barn and mule-stubborn. Saw her at an auction when I was seventeen and damn if I wasn't smitten right off. I begged my pa to buy her for the ranch, thought I couldn't be properly happy without her. We brought her home that night and the next morning I went out to ride her. You know, I can still remember how beautiful she looked that morning. I rubbed her down good and her coat was shining and her eyes were wide and alert, ready for a ride. I led her into the yard and the sun was just up on the horizon. Looking back, I don't think I've ever been so happy in my whole damn life.

"I swung up in the saddle, nice and easy, but before I could get my bearings, the Appaloosa bucked like she was on fire and I'll be damned if she didn't roll over like she'd been planning to murder someone all her life. I came out with only a pair of broken legs and a concussion, but that damn horse could've killed me on the spot."

A man shouted something at the other end of the bar. Clyde set his drink down.

"Sheriff, are you comparing my wife to a dangerous, bucking horse?"

"Guess that's up to you, Clyde."

Tyler smiled and studied the room. Both pool tables were still taken. George Jones sang about one more drink of wine on the jukebox. Tracy was joking with a table of older women, throwing her arms into the air as she told them something funny. An older couple was dancing on the small wood floor, ignoring everything but each other.

"Tyler, did you know Clyde sells insurance?"

"No, Sheriff. I didn't know that."

"Yes, sir. He'll sell you insurance, whether you need it or not."

Everybody laughed. Tyler grabbed his beer with his left hand, and his silver wedding band clinked against the glass. Clyde's head spun as if he'd been slapped and his bleary eyes widened.

"You're married."

"Yep," Tyler said. "Six years this past June."

"How's that going so far? Things still, you know, peaceable?"

"We're doing alright," Tyler said. "Hopefully this move will be good for us."

"Hear, hear," Merritt said. They all raised a glass and drank.

"So how did you two meet? If you don't mind me asking."

"Sure," Tyler said. "It was at a Cornhuskers game."

"Cornhuskers?"

"The football team," Merritt said. "The college football team. Shit, Clyde, how much have you had to drink?"

"Not enough," Clyde said. "Go on, Tyler. I didn't mean to interrupt."

"It was the Homecoming Game. We were playing Texas and I was in the pep band. We won the game on a last-second, thirty-five-yard pass play. Memorial Stadium went crazy. It was like an eighty-thousand-person stampede down to the field, a blur of red and white all around me. I lost my trumpet, but I didn't care. The crowd swept me along and we flowed toward the end zone where the team had scored.

"I ended up almost below the goalpost. A bunch of frat boys had already climbed the post and were doing their best to bring it down. The cheerleaders were there, too, cheering the frat boys on. The male cheerleaders began flipping the female cheerleaders into the air like potato chips into the mouth of a happy god, the happy god of Cornhusker football. Everyone was singing 'March of the Cornhusker' but I couldn't take my eyes off the flying cheerleaders. The way the sunlight turned their hair golden as they flew into the air was so beautiful, it freaking broke your heart."

Tyler paused and took a drink of beer.

"I don't know how it happened, maybe the crowd got too packed, or the guy cheerleaders got sloppy, but one of the cheerleaders was thrown off balance and I was the only one who noticed. I dove forward and caught her before she hit the ground. The cheerleader smiled and kissed my cheek, and, right there with the crowd cheering and clapping me on the back, I kissed her on the mouth, hard, and then we brought that goalpost to the ground. That was my wife. That was Anna."

SIX

The night had cooled, thank God. Anna walked with Bernie through the streets of Wormwood, keeping an eye out for the dog as they enjoyed the summer night. The neighborhood homes were softened by the darkness, their front yards blurred into a respectable hodgepodge of birdbaths, gnomes, and metallic animal sculptures. Sprinklers shot water across lawns, stuttering as they replaced the moisture stolen by the day. Dark figures sat rocking on their front porches, sipping from glasses as they watched the pedestrians walk by, occasionally raising their hands in salute.

Bernie lit a cigarette without breaking stride. Anna hadn't smoked since college, but she felt a sudden urge to bum a smoke. She'd like to draw that warm smoke into her lungs, that nicotine into her bloodstream, and let it loosen her tight limbs.

"You grew up in Nebraska, didn't you, Bernie? How'd you end up living so far west?"

Bernie smiled and tapped her cigarette. "I hitchhiked. Tyler's mother was only eleven at the time, but I was eighteen and sick of the Midwest. Our parents were pretty strict, too, and that wasn't much fun. So I packed a bag and headed out. Thought I'd go to Hollywood and be a star."

Bernie laughed. "You know, I expected the truckers I rode with to try something funny, but they acted like gentlemen, one and all. Just wanted some conversation, someone to joke with across all that interstate. Everything went easy as you please until Wormwood, when the trucker I was riding with had a heart attack while he was refueling his truck. After the ambulance picked him up, I saw a HELP WANTED sign outside the diner downtown and went inside, dead broke. They gave me a job as a short-order cook and it turned out I liked cooking, especially for a lot of people. Made me feel needed.

"I worked at the diner for about a year before a cafeteria position opened at the high school. The school system offered health benefits, higher pay, and more people to cook for, so I took the job, and I've worked there ever since. Not as glamorous as I thought my life would be, but I've had a good time over the years. They treat me well, and I get to work with all my friends. We call ourselves the Hairnets."

Bernie stopped. They'd reached Main Street. At least, the street sign said Main Street. It was hard to tell due to the utter lack of traffic. Across the street was the Mexican restaurant she and Tyler had passed on the way into town. Taco Thunder. The restaurant had its lights on, but the front parking lot was empty. Bernie stepped on her cigarette and blew out a stream of smoke. "Roscoe's partial to Mexican, but I don't see him sniffing around tonight. That means Merritt probably rounded him up already."

"Merritt?"

"Our sheriff. He's a real old-school type. Still rides a horse on patrol, packs a revolver. Nice, too. Couple of times he's brought Roscoe back to the house before I even knew the damn dog got loose."

"So—"

"Why don't we check the bar? It's Friday night, and the sheriff doesn't mind a drink now and then."

They walked a few blocks along Main Street. It was ten o'clock and the bar was the only lit thing on the entire street. They found Roscoe tied to a post outside a bar, keeping an old white horse company as he slurped water from a trough. When Bernie called the dog's name, Roscoe lifted his head and grinned, as if the entire evening had been a really fun game of hide-and-go-seek. Bernie scratched the shaggy dog behind the ears and scolded him at the same time. Anna stroked the horse's muzzle. It turned and peered at her with one brown eye.

"That's Sheriff Jackson's horse. Sadie."

Anna leaned her head against Sadie's neck. The horse's flesh was warm.

"I always wanted a horse like this."

"We should go in and thank the sheriff for finding Roscoe."

"Sure. Let's go in."

Anna patted the horse's neck good-bye. Sadie shook her head, her nostrils flaring as she sorted through the night wind.

They found the sheriff, every bit the gray-haired gunslinger Anna had imagined, sitting with Tyler and a slumped businessman in the middle of the packed bar. Tyler gave up his stool and stood in front of Anna, drinking a beer and nodding to the music. His eyes were bloodshot but still relatively clear. "So," Anna said, "you've been off having adventures with the town sheriff."

"Can you believe it? We rescued a dog."

"Amazing. You're a hero."

"I feel like a hero."

Anna smiled and ordered a cosmopolitan from the chesty brunette behind the bar. Bernie paid for Anna's drink, refusing all protests. As she took her first sip, Anna noticed the pool tables on the other side of the room. Two men waved their pool cues as they argued. The first man stopped paying attention to his cue and whacked a girl across the face. The girl screamed. The second man threw a punch, knocking the first man back onto the pool table. "Holy crap, Tyler," Anna said. "Do you see that?"

"What?"

"Those guys fighting."

Both men were on top of the pool table now, slugging each other. The girl, still grabbing the side of her face, screamed at both of them to stop. The first guy picked up the eight ball and brought it down on the second guy's face. Anna thought she heard the crunch all the way across the room, even with the music and crowd noise. That had to be a broken nose, at least. The man with the eight ball raised it above his head, ready to finish what he'd started, but as he brought his arm forward Merritt Jackson stepped out of the crowd and clocked him across the head with the butt of his gun, knocking the fighter flat on the table. Anna turned to the empty barstool beside her. The sheriff had been sitting there just a second ago, drinking his beer.

"Wow," Tyler said. "Did you see how he just stepped up like that? Wham! You sit down right now, motherfucker."

"How'd he get over there so fast?"

"Like he was taking out the trash. Didn't even pause."

Bernie leaned across from her stool. "He's good at stopping fights, isn't he? I think he's got some sort of sixth sense. Always seems to know when trouble's coming, and where it's going to happen."

"Sure," Tyler said. "Like Spiderman."

Anna took a drink. "Does this happen a lot around here? The fights?"

"Not too much," Bernie said, shrugging. "Once a month, maybe."

"Once a month?"

"Well. The heat gets to people."

Tyler slammed his glass on the bar. "The heat. Man. Did you *see* that?"

SEVEN

Tyler went over to see if the sheriff needed any help. Both fighters were still laid out on the table, one out cold, the other awake and pinching his nose, trying to stop the flow of blood. Merritt was talking to a woman who was also holding her face. Tyler stepped close, trying to listen in, but the woman was talking so fast he couldn't catch anything she said over the background noise. He drifted to the pool table. Tracy had brought a towel from the bar and was helping the conscious fighter press it against his nose. Tyler fingered the green felt on the pool table. Was there a way to get blood out of felt? Or would they have to re-cover the entire table? Tracy helped the conscious fighter off the table and sat him down in a chair. She made him tilt his head toward the ceiling and went back to the bar, leaving the towel. Tyler circled the pool table and lowered his head so it was level with the unconscious man. The man's mouth was open and he'd started to drool.

Merritt finished speaking with the woman and came over. He took off his hat and held it in his hands, revealing a close-cropped head of silver hair. "Chad, I'd like you to meet Tyler Mayfield." The sheriff chuckled and put his hat back on. "Guess Chad's not feeling too chatty right now."

"You know him?"

"Sure. He likes to come to the bar and shoot off his mouth. His brother Bobby usually keeps him in line, but he must not have come out tonight."

Tyler took a drink. "You going to leave him on the table until he wakes up?"

"Naw. He might not wake up until tomorrow. We'll put him outside and call his brother to pick him up."

"What were they fighting about?"

"The other fellow, Ryan, claimed Chad hit the eight ball prematurely. Chad didn't feel the same way. They got to arguing and Chad swiped Ryan's girl in the face with a pool cue. Probably an accident, but that was enough to get things started. Anyhow. You mind helping me with the prizefighter?"

Tyler set his glass down. He took Chad's feet and the sheriff took Chad's hands. They counted to three, lifted the man off the table, and set him on the barroom floor. He was heavy, like he'd been stuffed with clay. They took a breath and lifted Chad a few inches off the ground, the sheriff walking quickly backward as they made their way through the crowd. People stood back to let them pass, grinning as they watched the dangling man taken out. Anna appeared.

"Where are you taking him?"

"Outside," Tyler said. "He needs some fresh air."

Anna went ahead of them and held the door open. Tyler shifted his grip on Chad's boots. "Soon as we wrap up our official police business, I'll be back."

"Okay, Officer Mayfield. See you soon."

They sat the unconscious man down on a long bench that ran the length of the bar's wooden promenade. Chad slumped to the side, but didn't fully keel over. Merritt's shoulder mic squawked. The sheriff spoke into the mic in a low, undecipherable voice. Roscoe, still tied up beside the old white horse, barked at all of them and strained against his leash.

"Hate to put all this on you, Ty, but would you mind sitting with Chad a minute while I go back inside? Bobby should be here any minute to pick him up."

"Sure, sheriff. I don't mind."

"Appreciate it."

Merritt went back inside and a new batch of cigarette smoke poured out of the bar. Tyler crossed the promenade and scratched Roscoe behind the ears. He looked across Main Street to the east. The night sky was flooded with stars. Not much light pollution in central Nevada, just Las Vegas, around three hundred miles southeast.

The bar doors swung open. A man in a shirt and tie stumbled out, wavering uncertainly on the wooden promenade. He stopped, straightened his tie, and stumbled forward. "Tyler."

"Hey, Clyde. How's that gin treating you?"

"My wife left me today."

"That's what you said."

"Can you fucking believe that? She left."

Clyde lunged forward, aimed for the promenade railing, and missed it by a good foot. He fell to the ground and landed hard. He lay wheezing for a minute before getting to his knees and vomiting on the promenade's wooden boards. Tyler jumped back, not wanting to get it on his sandals. Clyde convulsed from the center of his gut, spraying out a salmon-colored soup that smelled like the ocean. Tyler watched the sky as he waited for Clyde to finish up, guessing which dots were stars and which were satellites. His brother had been into astronomy and could point out the constellations, even at different times of night, when they'd change with the earth's rotation. Cody said he'd learned astronomy to impress girls when they'd go on walks around Omaha, but Tyler knew he'd just said that to sound cool. His older brother had learned things like that because they simply existed, waiting to be learned. He'd been curious.

Clyde's stomach finished emptying and Tyler helped him stand up. The insurance agent moved slowly, as if he'd aged thirty years during the evening. Tyler set him on the bench next to the unconscious man and sat down himself. Clyde nodded.

"Evening, Chad."

"He's out, Clyde. He can't hear you."

"Oh," Clyde said, wiping his mouth. "He did seem kind of . . . slumped."

"Well. There was some punching."

Clyde leaned closer to Chad and snapped his fingers. "That was you fighting, huh, buddy? Disrupting the bar while the rest of us were trying to drink in peace? You fucking piece of trash."

"Easy there, Clyde."

"What? I'm right, aren't I? Just another hick in Hick Central. We should take his wallet. I'll split the cash with you."

"You're drunk, Clyde. You should go home and drink some water."

"Can't. The glasses are all dirty. Arleen left me a sink full of dirty dishes. Surprise, surprise."

"You could wash a glass."

"What? And let her win?"

Clyde tilted his head back against the bench. He breathed noisily through his mouth, staring out at the street. Tyler wondered what was taking Merritt so long. Anna would start thinking he'd gone home or something. And another beer wouldn't hurt anything, either. He'd had enough of this babysitting the drunk and concussed.

"That dog," Clyde said. "You see that dog over there?"

"Yeah?"

"He's eating my puke."

Tyler sat up. Clyde was right. Roscoe had found the liquid pile of vomit and was slurping it up like it was the world's greatest chili. Tyler thought about standing up and dragging the dog away from the puddle, but the thought alone was too exhausting. The dog was already half finished, anyhow. "If I had anything left to puke, I'd probably be back at it," Clyde said. "I mean, that's just disgusting."

Sadie whinnied and shook her head. Tyler looked up at the eastern sky and saw a bright light streaking through the stars. The light expanded until he could make out colors, red and yellow, with a thin blue edge. Moving fast, the light was headed toward town. Tyler stood and went to the railing. Clyde joined him.

"What the hell is that?"

"I don't know."

The night brightened. The buildings across the street threw shadows over the pavement, shadows that quickly grew tall and impossibly thin. "Oh," Clyde said, rubbing the side of his face.

The light disappeared. Something exploded nearby, shaking the earth. Tyler grabbed the railing to steady himself as his ears rang and bright swatches of color streamed across his vision. Roscoe barked spastically, straining at his rope. The sky boomed overhead, rattling every window downtown and setting off a frantic symphony of car alarms. In the distance, someone screamed themselves awake. Someone else shouted what the fuck is going on. A baby wailed. South down Main Street, a dirt-black mushroom cloud rose churning into the sky, dimming the orange street lamps along with everything else.

EIGHT

Anna checked the crowded bar's entrance for the seventh time, wondering what the heck was taking Tyler so long, and she'd just set her cosmo down when the explosion knocked it over.

It wasn't thunder. More like a bomb, exploding out on the street. It spilled drinks across the bar, sending beer, vodka, and soda into the laps of anyone not holding on to their glass. Nobody screamed or fell to the floor, but conversation ceased at exactly that instant. The crowd looked at one another, confused, and the only sound was Hank Williams yearning on the jukebox. Then the sky detonated like it'd been snapped in half, windows rattled in their frames, and half the bar's glassware, including dozens of liquor bottles behind the bar, crashed to the floor. Broken glass scattered everywhere and a woman screamed, grabbing her ankle. Anna got to her feet, remembering her nightmare from earlier that afternoon. If this was the end, she didn't want to be caught sitting on her ass.

Someone exhaled. Someone else laughed. Anna licked her lips and crossed her arms as conversation resumed in the bar. People filled the aisles, despite the broken glass. Merritt Jackson headed out the door, pressing his hat against his head as he spoke into his shoulder mic. Dazed, the bar crowd began to follow the sheriff, fumbling with their cell phones as they called home to check on their kids. Bernie stood beside Anna, hands on her hips.

"What do you think? Sounded like a car bomb."

Anna opened her mouth. Her ears rang as if she'd just left an AC/DC concert. Suddenly she knew.

"Something landed."

"Landed?"

"Yeah. A few blocks away."

The crowd was flowing steadily out the doors now. One man was pushing his way through in the opposite direction. Tyler.

Anna left Bernie and slipped into the crowd, using her hips to push her way through the excited mass of drunks. She met Tyler halfway, grabbed his hand, and pulled him along with her, back through the doors. Her husband was covered with soot. It ringed his eyes and sat thick on his eyelashes like cheap mascara. Anna had never seen his eyes so . . . open.

"Tyler?"

"I saw it. I saw it hit."

"What is it?"

"I don't know. It was bright. It lit up the whole sky. When I close my eyes, I can see colors."

"You're drunk."

"That doesn't matter. It lit up the sky."

The crowd ahead of them finally pushed through the doors. The air was dirtier outside than it'd been in the bar. Anna coughed and held her hand over her mouth. The horse wasn't tied to the post anymore. Neither was the dog. "That's the dirt cloud," Tyler said, squeezing her hand. "It got kicked up when it landed."

Anna coughed again. The people in front of them lowered their heads as they went up the street. The haze got thicker, and she could hardly see. It was like walking into a dirty blizzard. Atomic winter. Anna yanked her husband closer, until his hip brushed hers. "Don't let go of me, Ty. I can't see shit."

Foggy beams of light shone ahead. Flashlights. Or headlights. Anna realized the ringing in her ears was part car alarm. The security system of every damn automobile in town must have been set off by the crash. If they'd stayed in Nebraska, they'd be cuddling on the couch right now, watching movies in their apartment. Friday nights were usually movie nights, unless Tyler whined enough and got his way. Then it was *Star Wars* Monopoly night. Right now, even that didn't sound too bad.

More lights appeared ahead, clustered in one dense patch. The landing site. In the added light, they could make out the bar crowd staggering along through the haze, indistinguishable from zombies except for the fact several shouted into their cell phones, straining to be heard over the car alarms.

Anna dropped her hand and took a breath, clenching her teeth to keep the dust out.

"What's with this town, Tyler?"

Tyler squinted at the lights ahead. "I don't know, but I like it."

"You would. The weirder the better, with you. You're probably hoping Godzilla's up there, breathing fire and smashing buildings. That'd make your day, wouldn't it?"

"Hell, that'd make my life."

They closed the gap and came up to all the lights. The road changed from smooth pavement to cheap asphalt. They stepped off the street and onto a parking lot. Grit crunched beneath their shoes.

"Where are we?"

"I think this is Taco Thunder's parking lot."

"What?"

"The Mexican restaurant."

The crowd thickened again. Anna took over and led the way, wiggling through gaps, and they emerged on the other side. Anna exhaled. Over the last two days, they'd driven across Nebraska, Wyoming, Utah, and well into Nevada. They'd eaten two days' worth of fast food, forwarded their mail, said good-bye to their friends in Lincoln, packed most of their lives into one single Volvo, met a long lost relative, and witnessed a nasty bar fight. They'd done all this, and now, exhausted and sweaty, Anna and Tyler Mayfield found themselves staring at something even more fucked up than all that had come before.

NINE

The crater wasn't massive, but it had taken out a good chunk of ground. Anna guessed it was about seven feet deep and eight or nine feet across. A half-dozen flashlights were already trained on the pit, but she couldn't make out anything at its bottom. The dirty air was thick here, hanging over the crater like a storm cloud made of silt. People pressed in from behind as the crowd surged forward. Anna leaned back against the surge. She wasn't getting shoved into any crater tonight. No thank you.

"Tyler, help me push."

Tyler tested the edge of the crater with his foot, stomped on it a few times, and sat down, swinging his thin legs out into the empty air. He patted the ground beside him. "Have a sit. You won't have to worry about getting pushed in, and the air isn't so bad down here."

Anna crouched down. "The ground's dirty."

"We're all dirty. No use worrying about your clothes now."

"Are you sure it's safe?"

"Seems solid enough."

Anna tested the edge with her own foot. Nothing crumbled, so she sat down beside her husband. The air was slightly clearer down here. Most of the dirt must have still been high up, hanging above the parking lot. It would probably take hours, maybe days, for it to filter down again. Talk about bad air quality. You'd be able to feel it with a swipe of your hand.

Some men pushed their way through the crowd on the opposite side of the crater and began setting up equipment. Two halogen lamps snapped on, making Anna and the rest of the crowd wince. The duel lamps were set on top of a tripod, and the men aimed the lamps into the crater, illuminating it as if it were a Hollywood movie set. Anna shielded her eyes against the glare and studied the men behind the lamp. She could make out Sheriff Jackson with his cowboy hat and two other men in uniform. They conferred in a circle, ignoring the restless crowd behind them. The conference broke up and one of the men slipped back into the crowd. Sheriff Jackson raised his hands.

"Please, everyone. We'd appreciate it if you stepped back from the crater. We don't want anyone getting hurt. Give us ten yards of clearance and we'll get this dug out for a proper look."

The crowd murmured, pressing forward before reluctantly backing up. Tyler and Anna got to their feet and followed the crowd back to the new perimeter, which was actually more like two yards away from the crater than ten. Tyler wiped his mouth with the back of his hand. "You know what, I bet this is a hypervelocity crater. I saw this on *Nova* one time."

"Which means what?"

Tyler pointed to the crater. "That's a meteorite down there. A meteorite from outer space."

"Ah. Of course."

Two men carrying shovels emerged from the crowd. They sat on the edge of the crater and tossed their shovels into the pit. They slid in after their shovels and landed on their feet, knees bent to absorb the impact. They wore jeans, gray T-shirts, and yellow work boots. Anna would have bet a hundred dollars they were off-duty city workers, and a hundred on top of that that they'd been drinking at the bar with everyone else just fifteen minutes ago. The crowd pushed forward to watch. Anna and Tyler found themselves back where they'd started, right on the edge of the crater. The city workers picked up their shovels and started poking at the crater floor in short jabs, as if they expected to hit a land mine. Something clanged near the center of the crater. They began working in that area, shoveling fast. "They're never going to believe this back home," Tyler said, blowing into his hands. "A meteorite, landing right in the center of town."

"Maybe it'll be on the news."

"You think so? On the national news?"

"Why not? They've got to fill the time up somehow."

Tyler put his arm around her and squeezed. "That'd be

cool. I bet scientists are going to come from all over to study it. Maybe they'll want to interview people about it. I saw it fall."

"Maybe you'll be on the news."

"You think so?"

The city workers shoveled off more dirt. Even with the halogen lamps, it was hard to make out the rock against the soil, with the air so hazy around it. Their shovels rang occasionally, glancing off the rock. The more they shoveled, the bigger the rock grew, and soon they'd dug out the area around it entirely. The crowd's hum grew louder as the city workers stood back and leaned against their shovels, their faces so dirty Anna couldn't tell if they were smiling or frowning. Almost triangular, the rock had a smooth, curved face and a flat bottom. It reminded Anna of the type of skipping stone you hoped to find on the shore of a lake.

"Imagine how old it is," Tyler said. "How far it must of come to land here on earth. You know, some meteors have been sailing around since the big bang."

"You really think that's a meteorite down there, Tyler?"

Her husband grinned and nodded, the left side of his face hidden in shadow. Anna shivered and rubbed her bare arms. She didn't like that look. She didn't like this meteorite, either. It had a way of pulling at you.

For one hundred fifty years, scientists have studied meteorites with the knowledge that they are rocks from space. These small bodies have led some of us on a journey to know ourselves. They have been responsible, in part, for our origins and, in part, for the demise of our animal ancestors. They are why we are here.

—O. Richard Norton, *Rocks from Space*

BOOK II

THE STREWN FIELD

TEN

Particles of dirt and sand sifted down through the air, still settling from the impact as word of the meteorite spread through Wormwood. People threw jackets over their pajamas and clomped to the landing site, dragging sleepy children by the hand to witness history. By midnight the scene at the crater was downright festive, and Tyler Mayfield enjoyed every second of it. He drank from a bottle of tequila making the rounds and chatted with the locals, trying to remember everything he could about meteors while Anna smiled without commenting and watched the crowd. A tall man in a sombrero was grilling hot dogs in the parking lot, handing them out to whoever passed by and waving off attempts at payment. Dogs ran around Main Street, chasing one another. Parents shouted at their children, ordering them to stay away from the pit, goddamn it.

They'd found Mr. Diaz, the owner of Taco Thunder, tossed into a Dumpster three blocks away. He was in shock, but alive. Bernie knew the Diaz family well, and she left in a hurry to drive to the Silverton Hospital, where she planned to spend the night with Rosa and her daughters. If this wasn't crazy enough, a news van had shown up on the edge of the crowd to film the crater and interview eyewitnesses. A reporter and her cameraman had jumped into the crowd and now they reappeared, followed by a man covered in soot. The reporter, a petite brunette in her late twenties, wore a sharp burgundy suit coat and a black skirt that stopped an inch above her knees. She was pretty, Anna thought, but not that pretty. Her eyebrows were too close together, and she scowled at the camera like she was about to bite it. Anna could have stood in front of a camera like that, asking a few easy questions while she glowed for the viewers at home. She could have done it with better posture, too.

Tyler hugged Anna from behind and peered over her shoulder. "Hey, isn't that Clyde Ringston?"

"Who?"

"That guy they're interviewing. That's Clyde."

"Who's Clyde?"

"That guy we were sitting next to at the bar. In the shirt and tie."

"The drunk sad guy?"

"Yep. That's him. And now he's going to be on TV."

"Jesus," Anna said. "Wormwood gets one person to represent it, and it's the drunk sad guy?"

The cameraman's bright light went out. The interview was over. The tech guy wrapped cables around his forearm while the reporter and Clyde stood outside the van talking for another minute. Clyde took a step back from the reporter, held his hand up in good-bye, and returned to the crowd. The reporter noticed Anna watching and returned her stare. The cameraman got into the van and slammed the driver's-side door. The reporter jumped at the loud noise, dropping her gaze. She got into the van's passenger seat and shut her door, staring straight ahead. Anna watched the van's taillights as it headed out of town, already on the way to the next interesting destination, the next story.

Anna turned to her husband. "Let's go home, Ty."

"What? Why?"

"I'm tired."

"You're tired? The party's just getting started. I just saw someone with a new bottle of tequila."

"I don't care. This is too much. People shouldn't act like this. It's weird."

Tyler looked around. "Act like how?"

"This isn't a party. A meteorite landed and almost killed someone and they're acting like it's fucking New Year's Eve times a hundred. It's only a matter of time until somebody takes off their clothes."

"So? They're blowing off steam. What's wrong with that?"

Anna sighed and ran her hand through her matted, dust-clotted hair. "I don't know. I guess I'm just tired."

Two silent children ran past them, gray with dirt. One of the city workers who'd dug up the meteorite whipped off his shirt, spun it over his head, and whooped as he threw it into the polluted sky. Anna sighed and crossed her arms.

"See?"

ELEVEN

They found Roscoe waiting for them at home, curled up and snoring in front of the gate. The dog looked even dirtier than they did, if that was possible, and he still had Merritt's lasso hanging around his neck, the rope end chewed off about a foot down. Tyler woke the dog up and led him inside the yard, swatting the dirt from his fur like it was a Persian carpet. Anna watched Tyler work, smiling, and when the dog was tolerable they went inside.

"I'm going to take a shower and go to bed," Anna said, stretching her arms out. "You coming with me, dirty boy?"

"That's okay," Tyler said. "I'm still too keyed up. You go on without me."

"Alright, sweetie. Good night."

"Night."

Tyler listened to his wife go upstairs and went into the kitchen. He found the liquor and poured himself a shot of whiskey. He downed the shot, hissed through his teeth, and set the shot glass in the sink. He went back to the living room and paced, kneading the shag carpeting with his toes. He checked the grandfather clock in the corner of the room. Two A.M.

"What do you think, Roscoe? Time for TV?"

The dog yawned and left the room. Tyler could hear the metal buckle on the dog's collar clinking against his porcelain food dish. He looked around for the TV remote but couldn't find it. He noticed a built-in bookshelf above the picture of Leonard Nemoy. The shelf was lined with old encyclopedias that had blue cloth covers and a strip of black on each spine, so that when the books were aligned together the individual strips of black created a chunky line. Tyler took the letter M off the shelf. He sat down on the sofa and opened the book on his lap. Roscoe returned from the kitchen and sat at his feet, whapping the carpeted floor with his tail. Tyler found the entry for meteors and began to read the page-long entry.

Apparently, the light he and Clyde had seen while standing outside the bar had been the meteor entering the earth's atmosphere and encountering friction. The friction caused the meteor's surface to catch fire and change shape, a process called ablation. The encyclopedia entry claimed most meteors broke up at this point, while still in the upper atmosphere, and that's what created the light of a falling star. Even meteors that made it to the earth relatively intact (like the Wormwood meteorite) often shed some of their mass during the ablation process, throwing bits of rock across their descent path, creating what was called a strewn field. Sometimes, you could find over a thousand meteorite fragments in one area.

Tyler set the encyclopedia beside him on the couch. There could be more pieces of meteorite outside of town, waiting to be found. All of Wormwood could be considered a strewn field now. This was something to consider. This required a more philosophical state of mind.

"Roscoe."

The dog's ears perked up.

"You want to go outside?"

The dog laid his head on his paws and shut his eyes. Tyler left the dog to his beauty sleep and went out alone.

Two years after Cody Mayfield went missing, Tyler's family held a letting-go ceremony for the missing teenager. It was his mother's idea. She'd read about letting-go ceremonies in one of her books on coping with child loss and grief. Tyler hated those books. They didn't know what the fuck they were talking about. Those books were nothing but a collection of words slapped together by some Ph.D. trying to make a few extra bucks in the lucrative nonfiction market. Okay, sometimes their authors told personal stories of their own loss, but why should he care about them? They hadn't known Cody. They'd only known some dork in their own lives. It wasn't the same thing.

They held the letting-go ceremony on the second anniversary of Cody's disappearance. His mother sent out formal invitations to family members and a dozen of Cody's friends from school, and everyone, every single person, showed up.

Tyler expected the ceremony to be held somewhere scenic, on the shore of a rippling lake, or in a windy state park somewhere, but his mother surprised him and they held the ceremony in the parking lot of the Westroads Mall.

A podium was placed on the edge of the mall parking lot. It was a late Sunday afternoon and the lot was about half full. Most of the cars were parked near the mall and their stretch of parking lot was empty except for a single VW Bug, its lime green body glinting in the sunlight in a way that made Tyler feel queasy. While his mother walked through the crowd, greeting each person in turn, Tyler's father set up a folding table beside the podium and set out several photo albums on the table, arranging them chronologically with the fussiness of a miniaturist. One of his father's friends from work had brought an enormous plastic cooler stuffed with ice, beer, and soft drinks. The crowd drifted from his mother to the table, consoling his father while they picked out a beverage. Tyler stayed apart from the crowd. He didn't want a drink from the cooler, no matter how hot the stupid parking lot was.

Before the ceremony started, mall cops showed up in their mall buggy. They wore stiff white uniforms and dark sunglasses. His mother brought the mall cops each a Coke and chatted with them, smiling and touching her hair. After a minute, they got back in their mall buggy and drove away, going maybe five miles an hour. His mother returned to the podium. She spoke without a microphone and thanked everyone for coming. The crowd remained standing because no one had brought chairs. She told a funny story about Cody on Christmas morning, and then she invited someone else to come up and talk. Tyler looked the other way as a girl he'd never seen before told a story about how Cody helped her out in art class. Waves of watery air hovered over the gray pavement. An SUV drove past, blaring Pearl Jam. The voice changed up front, telling another story about Cody, also mentioning how sweet and awesome he was.

Wow.

Big whoop.

A jet plane flew by, about two thousand feet overhead. Tyler made his hand a gun and shot it down. He imagined the panicked pilot, fighting for control of the plane as it plunged through the atmosphere. The pilot hits the eject button, but something jams. The ground rises up fast now. The pilot says an old prayer his grandmother taught him when he was a little boy. He sees a gray city rise up in the middle of a green Nebraska. Then a mall inside that city, and a half-empty parking lot around that mall. With one last violent pull on the controls, the pilot manages to steer the plane away from the mall and toward the parking lot. Too late, he sees the crowd of people gathered at the end of the parking lot. The plane plows right into their podium and explodes. Bodies fly everywhere.

The voices went on and on, talking about his brother. Tyler turned around only when they'd finished, an oddly expectant hush falling over the crowd. His father was holding up a copy of Laser Slash IV, the video game his brother had gone to the mall to buy. The game was still in its wrapper.

His father held up a plastic lighter, thumbed a small flame into life, and set the game on fire. The plastic wrapper caught right away. His father dropped the game on the parking lot and stepped back as the flames grew around it. You could smell the plastic burning.

Someone in the crowd started humming. Someone else joined in, and suddenly the entire crowd of thirty white corn-fed Nebraskans began singing a tremulous, off-key rendition of "Amazing Grace." His mother wept as his father hugged her against his paunch. Tyler headed for the minivan, keeping his eyes on the parking lot's pavement.

Bernie's backyard reminded Tyler of a haphazard Japanese rock garden. The tall wooden fence hid the yard from neighbors. Small boulders littered the yard, placed with no apparent rhyme or reason, and decorative objects sat on top of many of the rocks, like kitschy offerings to the gods. Tyler made his way through the maze slowly, with the help of the backdoor light, and sat on a bench swing at the rear of the yard. He spread the blanket he'd brought over his lap. The bench was chained to the sort of wide, four-legged frame used in parks for children's swing sets, with each leg cemented in a concrete anchor. The chains creaked as Tyler pushed off the ground and set the bench in motion.

A bat dipped into the yard, swooped in erratic circles, and flew off again. Tyler dug into his pocket and pulled out a pack of cigarettes and a plastic lighter. He opened the pack and pulled out a white paper tube thinner than a standard-sized cigarette. He ran the joint beneath his nose and inhaled its acrid-sweet smell, pinching it to make sure it was still rolled tight. He lit the joint and inhaled, allowing the smoke to roll through his chest and carry upward into the tense pockets of his mind.

Tyler took another pull and studied Bernie's strange garden. On top of one boulder was a steer's skull, horns and all. Perched on another boulder was an owl, carved out of wood and perfectly still. He could also make out a man's black marble head, a copper cat, and a sundial that glowed chalky white, as if it had stored the sun's energy throughout the day and now radiated it back into the night. Tyler blew a curl of smoke out the side of his mouth and knocked the ash off his joint. "*Très* spooky," he said, and laughed at the sound of his own voice. One of these boulders might have been part of the meteor, he realized. Or one of the smaller rocks, the ones that didn't have any lawn ornaments on top of them. Strewn field. This whole town was one big strewn field.

The bench's chains squeaked as Tyler tilted backward. His limbs floated above him, filled with helium and tethered by invisible filaments of space-time. Nevada lifted around him, rendered so full of meaning as to lose all meaning. He was standing in front of a cosmic chalkboard, telling every star in the universe about the collective works of F. Scott Fitzgerald and why they mattered so much, even at this scale. The stars continued burning and made no response.

The bench stopped swinging. He'd forgotten to push. Tyler opened his eyes to look for the ground and saw instead a round gray face peering at him from behind one of the rock garden's boulders. The face's dark, liquid eyes were shaped like almonds and slanted inward. Its nose was missing. Its mouth was a thin, wrinkled line, and its head was shaped like a balloon.

Tyler squinted his vision together, convinced the face would disappear upon closer inspection, but it remained in the garden. He'd seen those eyes earlier that day in the rearview mirror, on the way into Wormwood.

Tyler opened his mouth and took a short, tentative breath. The face's expression didn't change, so he took another breath, and a third. The oxygen gradually made its way back into his bloodstream. The joint burned down between his fingers, forgotten. Anna would never believe him.

"Hello," Tyler said. "How are you tonight?"

The figure's mouth twitched into a wrinkle and smoothed out again. Tyler didn't know what that was supposed to mean.

"Did you land with the meteorite?"

The figure ducked down and disappeared behind one of the boulders. He'd been too forward.

"Please. Don't go. I'm sorry. I'll shut up."

Tyler waited, but the figure did not reappear. He took a last drag on the joint and toed it into the dirt, where it could rest with dozens of his aunt's cigarette butts. A coyote howled somewhere west of town, off in the mountains. Tyler stood up, stretched, and walked back through the garden, eyeing the boulders for signs of movement. He wondered if the figure had ever been there in the first place, or if he'd hallucinated the whole thing. It was possible.

It had been a long day.

TWELVE

The next morning Anna woke curled in a fetal position, somewhere dark and not her bed. Her pillow was bundled, dirty, and denim. Jeans. She'd been drooling into the crotch of somebody's blue jeans. The only light visible was a thin whip of brightness along the floor. The air was musty. Overhead, almost brushing her face, hung several tops and dresses. She pushed the closet door with her hand and it slid open along its track. She winced at the flood of daylight and crawled forward, her hands sticking to the glossy cover of a magazine as she pushed herself off the floor and stood up. Her entire body was greasy with sweat and matted hair. Lovely. Anna went into the bathroom and washed her face, twice, and threw on some clean clothes. She found Tyler in the dining room, sitting in front of an empty plate as he read the newspaper.

"Morning, sunshine. You want some French toast?"

"Where's Bernie?"

"She just went to bed. She sat up with the Diaz family all night. Mr. Diaz is okay. They're bringing him home this afternoon."

Anna sat down at the table.

"Let me get a plate for you."

Anna watched her husband as he left the room and went into the kitchen. He was so skinny. Too skinny. Was he skinnier than her now? That wouldn't be good. She probably reminded people of a cow, walking around with him.

Tyler returned with a plate of French toast and a cup of coffee.

"I woke up on the closet floor, Ty."

"What? I didn't know you sleepwalked."

"I don't. I mean, normally." Anna cut into the eggy bread with the edge of her fork. "I had a nightmare, too. Something about an earthquake cracking the earth in half, like it was a freaking egg."

Tyler rubbed her back with the palm of his hand. "You're probably stressed out. Moving is very stressful. Actually, I'm surprised I'm not having messed-up dreams, too."

"Sure," Anna said. "Stress dreams."

"New environment, new people, new house."

Anna pushed her French toast around. "And that meteor landing downtown last night. What was the deal with that?"

"I don't know. That was pretty surreal, though."

"There's something strange about that meteorite."

"Like how?"

"I don't know."

"It's from outer space. That's strange."

"That's not what I mean. It has a . . . presence."

"Maybe it's here to invade our town," Tyler said, pushing his chair back from the table. "We should all start carrying loaded firearms. Alert the U.S. military. Sweep the perimeter."

Anna chewed her food and stared at her husband. Tyler held up his hands and bugged out his eyes.

"What? I thought we were trying to brainstorm here."

"You know," Anna said, tapping her fork on the edge of her plate, "in horror movies, the smart-ass usually dies first."

Later that day Anna and Bernie drove across town to the Diaz household to deliver a tray of get-well-soon lemon bars. They found the entire family standing outside their beige ranch-style house despite the heat, arguing around a ratty brown recliner. Bernie parked on the street and turned off the car. She pointed out Rosa Diaz and her two teenage daughters, Angela and Izel. "The Diaz family likes to argue," Bernie said. "Don't worry. This scene is nothing unusual. Just more outdoors."

Rosa shouted at Mr. Diaz, waving her thick arms wildly, as if she was about to haul off and bitch-slap someone.

"We could come back," Anna suggested. "When things have cooled down."

"Ha," Bernie said, opening her door. "If I waited for things to cool down around here, I'd never get to visit."

They got out of the car. Anna carried the lemon bars. They'd made her lap overheat on the way over and she'd plucked at her shorts, trying to get some airflow down south. Mr. Diaz was standing behind the recliner, with both hands on the headrest. His wife, Rosa, a short, plump Mexican American woman with wide hips and black hair hanging loose down to the middle of her back, was standing in front of the recliner with her feet planted firmly apart. Her blood-shot eyes darted to each member of her family, trying to watch everyone at once. Angela and Izel stood on either side of the recliner, arms crossed and faces chubby with lingering baby fat. Neither girl was ugly, but with their inherited genetics, it was obvious they didn't have much of a shot at becoming drop-dead gorgeous. Anna felt an urge to pluck Angela's bushy unibrow and order Izel to stop slouching. She fell in step behind Bernie, allowing the lunch lady to walk point.

"Hey, everybody. What's going on?"

Rosa glanced at them and moved over, letting them into the ring. "Good. Bernie's here. Maybe she can help talk some sense into you, you crazy old man. Will you listen to her?"

"I do not need to discuss this matter with Bernie."

"Discuss what matter, Charles?"

"He's bringing his recliner to the crater," Angela said. "He says he needs to assume his post."

"Your post?"

"Moses had his mountain. I shall have the meteor crater."

"Like hell you're going downtown," Rosa said, hands on her hips. "Do you want to kill yourself? You need to be resting your poor brain, not sitting out in this heat. Moses wasn't a victim of brain trauma."

Mr. Diaz squeezed the recliner's headrest so hard the tips of his fingernails turned white. "I'm not going to argue with you, Rosa. This is what I'm going to do. Do not hinder me."

"Moses?" Bernie said. "What about Moses?"

"My husband thinks he's a prophet suddenly. One trip across the sky and he's Joan of Arc."

Izel snickered and stroked the recliner's arm, as if it were a live animal.

"Tell them," Rosa said. "Tell them your prophecy, Joan."

Mr. Diaz wiped the sweat off his upper lip. He stared straight ahead, as if he could no longer see his wife.

"C'mon, Charles. You want to spread the word, don't you? Start with these two. They're listening."

Izel circled around the chair and stood beside her sister. Anna shifted the lemon bars to her hip.

"The end is near," Mr. Diaz said. "The Meteor is approaching."

Anna curled a ringlet of her hair around her finger.

"The Meteor?"

"Yes. The World-Ender. The All-Destroyer."

The Diaz girls looked at each other. No more smirks now.

"So you had a vision," Bernie said. "When the meteor hit the parking lot. You had a vision of a giant meteor hitting earth."

"No. No vision."

Anna shifted the tray to her other hip. She could actually

feel her skin growing more sunburned as they stood in the driveway.

"What was it, then? A dream?"

"No. No dream. When I woke up in hospital, I just knew. I felt the Meteor's approach in my bones. I can feel it now, growing nearer by the minute as it hurtles through the vacuum of space."

Rosa clucked her tongue. "You see what I mean? Crazy. Suddenly he cares so much about outer space."

"I did a science project on the solar system once," Angela said, turning to Anna. "He didn't help with shit."

"Angela," Bernie said. "Watch your tongue."

"But it's true. He didn't."

Mr. Diaz was finished with debate. He rearranged his grip on the recliner and began dragging it across the driveway. The recliner's wooden feet scraped on the pavement and the Diaz girls covered their ears. Anna set the pan of lemon bars on the hot driveway, tired of holding them.

Rosa ran up and sat in the recliner. "You leave this driveway, don't plan on coming back, Charles."

"Get out of my chair."

"I'm serious. I grew up with a crazy uncle. I don't want any of that crap around my daughters. Teenagers need a good, stable environment. Not some Mexican Chicken Little."

Mr. Diaz grabbed the chair at its base and tipped his wife onto the lawn. She landed on her hands and knees and rolled into a sitting position. Angela ran over, but Rosa ignored her daughter's hand.

"You need help, Charles. Help."

"The whole world needs help, Rosa. The whole world needs to be warned before it is too late."

Mr. Diaz crawled the recliner onto the sidewalk, occasionally bumping it along with his stomach. His chest heaved and sweat ran down his unshaven cheeks. He looked like a man working on a heart attack, a thrown-out back, and a stroke, all in one afternoon. Izel followed her father down the sidewalk, glancing back every few yards as she hovered around the recliner. Finally, the girl ran back and sat beside Rosa on the lawn. Rosa leaned against her younger daughter's shoulder and wept. Angela pretended she couldn't hear her mother crying and stepped into the street, watching her father crabwalk the chair to the next block, slowly heading west.

Bernie lit a cigarette and took a drag. She blew the smoke through her nose.

"Well. That's different."

Anna retrieved the tray of lemon bars from the smoldering pavement. No doubt they'd melted into a puddle of lemon filling and powdered sugar by now. She slid the cover off, expecting the worst.

THIRTEEN

For the first few days following the meteorite's landing, Wormwood's residents converged on the fall site en masse. When residents weren't working or sleeping, you could find them in Taco Thunder's parking lot, sitting in lawn chairs or milling about in an excited crowd. Scientists showed up from Arizona State and the University of New Mexico to photograph the meteorite and ask everyone to describe the event, even folks who hadn't actually seen it land and had only shown up later for the party. The scientists estimated the meteorite's weight at around two to three tons and its composition to be almost entirely nickel iron, which explained how it had survived entering the earth's atmosphere and plunging through seven feet of sandy, asphalt-coated soil.

The locals didn't care much about the details, though. What mattered to them was the mind-boggling fame the landing had brought to the town, the notoriety in the local and national press. Not only had the meteorite landing been seen on the NBC, ABC, and CBS evening news, there had even been a segment on it on the *Today* show. Nothing even close to this much action had ever blown through town. Some spoke of Area 51 in hushed tones, suggesting the creation of a gift shop, a mini-putt course, even a town tourism bureau. The mayor, a chain-smoking Persian Gulf veteran named Jim Lockstead, suggested that if Wormwood played its cards right the event could be parlayed into heaps of money, commercial development, a major chain restaurant. Suddenly the future wasn't in the stars; it had come down from the stars, landing smack in the middle of Taco Thunder's parking lot like a gift from the economic gods.

As for Taco Thunder itself, the Mexican restaurant was up and running again despite the fact that it was now totally ignored by Mr. Diaz. While his wife and daughters labored to keep up with the increased business, Charles Diaz spent his days sitting at the edge of the crater and watching the sky. He'd fashioned a sign using white poster board and red marker, stenciling THE END IS NEAR in thick, block letters across the board. He sat at all times with the board on his lap, maintaining a quiet vigil while the rest of town buzzed around him. He got up only to use the Taco Thunder bathroom and ate only when Rosa brought out something from the restaurant. Their conversations took on a familiar pattern that went well with the frenzied atmosphere of downtown Wormwood.

"Charles, put that sign down."

"I will put this sign down when the time comes to lay everything down."

"Please, Charles. At least put it down long enough to eat some lunch. I brought you chicken tacos today. Make sure you clean your plate this time. You're getting thin."

"I will lay the sign at my feet, but the words will still be there."

"Okay. Whatever. Take the plate."

"Thank you."

"You're welcome. You should see how hard our daughters are working while you sit staring into the sky. Any chance you'd be willing to come inside and help?"

"No. This is my place now. The only place that matters."

The university scientists begged to have samples of the meteorite donated to their schools. This was Mr. Diaz's decision, since the meteorite had fallen on his land, and while he allowed small samples to be taken from the meteorite, he announced that the rock would never be removed from the site, not for any amount of money. He also refused to talk about extricating the rock and repairing the parking lot. The meteorite would stay where it had fallen until the end of the world, which wasn't very far off, if you'd been paying attention.

The meteorite landing didn't stop summer school, though, and the following Monday Tyler Mayfield showed up to Wormwood High early for the first day of class. The school had been built in the early 1970s. It sat on the northeast edge of town, just beyond the last residential homes. Shaped like a capital E, its three wings pointed west, toward the mountains.

The school's exterior was the type of red sandstone brick usually reserved for fire halls or minimum-security prisons. The building was dotted with windows, four to a classroom, and each window was heavily tinted against the Nevada sun. Tyler found his classroom for the next ten weeks and skimmed his lesson plan before laying his head down on his desk, arms crossed for a pillow. His face felt hot. A contract had been signed, and this was his trench for the foreseeable future. No more slumming from school to school, substituting for teachers with bad backs, pregnant bellies, dead relatives, and clogged arteries. His contract was only for one year, but who knew? They could offer him another contract. He simply needed to do a competent job and win the respect of his peers. It couldn't be that hard, could it?

His class filed in around eight o'clock and sat down, choosing their seating arrangement for the next ten weeks. Tyler tried to make eye contact and smile at all ten students, even the pimply kid with the lazy eye, hoping they'd soon come to understand that his classroom was going to be a safe, egalitarian society where ideas sprang to life with effortless fluidity. "Hello, class," Tyler said, going with a classic power opening. "My name is Tyler Mayfield, and this is remedial composition."

A few students nodded. Tina, a blond girl who was chewing gum and wearing an improbable red beret, held up her hand.

"Yes?"

"Your last name is Mayfield?"

"You got it."

"What kind of name is that? Are you Indian or something?"

"No, I'm not. I'm Armenian Italian. My great-grandfather decided to change his name when he came to this country, and he picked Mayfield."

"He sounds crazy," a Mexican kid said from the second row. "Was he crazy?"

"Not that I know."

Tina pursed her lips and adjusted her beret. "Armenian? Are you sure? You look sort of Mexican to me."

"He's not Mexican," the Mexican kid said. "No way."

The day went downhill from there. He hadn't expected his new students' foul moods to be so entrenched, their distrust of him to be so deeply engrained. It was as if they'd been told their entire lives that one dark day they'd meet a new teacher from another state, the state of Nebraska, perhaps, and that the only reasonable response to an out-of-state teacher like this would be to make his job as hard as possible. In fact, the only glimmer of genuine interest Tyler received all day was when he'd mentioned the meteorite landing.

"You saw it land?"

"Not exactly. But I was at the crater about five minutes later."

"What did it look like?"

"Lots of dirt in the air."

"Dirt?"

"It hung like a muddy cloud above the parking lot. People

had to hold their shirts over their faces so they could breathe. It reminded me of camera footage from war zones."

Another student, a square-faced junior who had introduced himself to the room as "Skull" and was dressed from head to toe in black, raised his hand. He had a silver nose ring connected to an ear piercing by a classy silver chain.

"Did you see Mr. Diaz go flying into the air? I bet he looked like some sort of fat, freaky bird."

"No, I didn't."

"I heard Diaz sits by the crater all day long," Skull said, leaning over his desk and looking at the room. "All night, too. He hardly ever sleeps. He says that the meteorite downtown is just the start. There's another meteor coming to destroy the world. Bigger than the one that killed all the dinosaurs."

"Yes," Tyler said. "That's what he's saying. But—"

"Sounds like he's gone nutso," Tina said. "Someone should dust off a straitjacket for him, if they can find one that big."

The students laughed.

"Alright, people," Tyler said, turning back to the marker board. "Let's get back on track."

Skull stopped by Tyler's desk after class. Tyler noticed Skull's dark hair was tied in a ponytail that hung down to the middle of his back. That took dedication: The kid must have been growing his hair out since he was twelve.

"What do you think, Mr. Mayfield?"

"About what, Skull?"

"Is Mr. Diaz crazy?"

"He was in shock. That would scramble anyone's mind for a while."

"So you think he's wrong about the super meteor?"

"I hope so."

Skull shrugged and looked out through the tinted classroom windows. "Yeah. Probably. But it'd be pretty cool to see, though, wouldn't it?"

"I guess. Until the meteor actually hit the earth, anyway."

Skull nodded and started toward the door. "See you tomorrow, Mr. Mayfield. Only nine weeks and four days left."

Tyler hit the bar on his way home from school. He sat on a stool beside Clyde Ringston, who leaned on the bar with his elbows and stared into a tumbler filled with gin. Clyde breathed slowly, his stomach pushing against his white dress shirt. Besides Stan, the daytime bartender, Tyler and Clyde were the only people in the bar. The bar's jukebox was silent. Stan stood with his arms crossed at the other end of the bar, watching a courtroom show on TV. You could hear the defendants making their outrageous claims, though what came across to Tyler was more of a sense of cloudy ignorance than sentences that actually made sense when strung together. The daytime bartender smoked a cigarette as he watched the show, sometimes laughing, then coughing.

"How you been, Clyde?"

"Okay. My wife called me."

"Oh yeah?"

"She saw me interviewed on the news. She wanted to know what Shyla Collins was like in person. I told her she smelled like cherries and vanilla."

Tyler took another drink. The beer tasted a little sour, as if someone had added lemon juice to it. He took another drink and decided it wasn't too bad. Smoke from Stan's cigarette drifted down the bar and hovered around them, masking the bar's locker-room scent. Clyde traced a figure eight on the bar with his finger.

"She asked if I wanted to have coffee."

"Coffee? Coffee's not too bad."

"Shit. Coffee. We lived together for twenty-five years, and now it's a big deal if we sit in the diner and drink coffee?"

"So what did you say?"

"I said I needed to think about it."

"Think about coffee?"

Clyde cleared his throat and coughed. "I don't know. It's kind of nice having the house to myself. I've been to her sister's place, and that woman is no picnic. I'm thinking maybe I should let her cool her heels for a few more days, let her think about how cozy she's had it with me."

Tyler picked at the wrapper on his bottle. "She could change her mind, you know. She could decide to have coffee with someone else."

Clyde smiled. "Well, Ty, that's a risk I'm willing to take."

Stan took the remote out of his shirt pocket and turned the TV volume up. On the screen a solemn guy in a cheap suit was interviewing an enormous woman in a knitted top. Mascara ran down the big woman's cheeks, and she stared at the camera in an imploring way that made Tyler look somewhere else. Clyde hunched over his drink and fell quiet, and in a few minutes it was as if they'd never spoken in the first place. The afternoon passed away in a golden, smoky haze. Tyler thought about going home soon. He ordered another beer and Stan brought it over.

Clyde raised his head. "You hear what they're thinking about?"

"Nope."

"They might change Wormwood Days."

"Wormwood Days?"

Clyde frowned at the TV. "Our annual street carnival. Usually happens at the end of August. They get rides for the kids, open up a beer garden on Main Street. Couple of country bands on stage. Some food vendors. You know, my favorite's fried doughnuts. You can stand and watch them make 'em right there in front of you."

"Sounds fun. I love a good beer garden."

"It's alright."

"So, how are they thinking about changing it?"

Clyde turned on his stool and pointed his drink at Tyler. "The mayor wants to call it Meteorite Days. Says the name will draw a bigger crowd. Get people to come in from all over, see the meteorite and spend some money. The mayor gets a bee in his bonnet and now a hundred years of history can go take a flying leap. You know what I mean, Ty?"

"Sure. That's terrible, man. You should protest it."

Clyde rubbed his jaw and stared red-eyed at the brass bar rail. "Yeah. Maybe I will. Maybe I'll protest."

Tyler drank the rest of his mediocre beer. The clock on the wall said three o'clock. Not even happy hour yet, and he felt a buzz coming on. The students in his remedial composition class drifted through his thoughts. Seven boys, three girls. All of them with that hungry, bored look. By the end of the day, they all had reminded Tyler of his brother in some way or another. Any of them could have been Cody reincarnated. It had been that long. He'd been gone for fifteen and a half years. Sometimes Tyler couldn't even remember what his older brother looked like, exactly, or how his voice sounded. A thirty-two-year-old Cody could walk into this bar right now, order a whiskey sour, and Tyler might not know him from Cain.

Hello, class. Welcome to Remedial Family, 101. Please open your books and turn them to chapter 1: "You Don't Even Know How Many Ways Your Loved Ones Can Cause You Pain."

FOURTEEN

Anna began working at the Lucky Coyote casino a week after they arrived in Wormwood. She flitted between the rows of slot machines, enjoying their continuous electronic chirping while she asked their glassy-eyed operators if they needed a drink. The machines were all so colorful, so bright with back-lit hope, that she could imagine any one of them paying out at any moment in a glorious clatter of quarters or, best of all, in a wailing jackpot siren, the screen flashing as the operator waited for the floor manager to come by and arrange payment beyond what could reasonably be collected in change. The reverie created by the machines and the general contented lull of the casino itself, a place lacking clocks and frequented by people without schedules, allowed Anna to spend her days dreaming of how she and Tyler would spend the money they'd save during their stay in Wormwood. They'd move back to Nebraska and buy a nice two-story Colonial, with at least two full bathrooms. They'd buy something near downtown Lincoln, so they could walk to restaurants in the historic district. They'd have a backyard and a gas grill so they could throw parties for their old university friends, complete with tiki torches and coolers brimming with Lite beer. She'd invite the girls she'd known on the cheer squad and they'd bring their stocky, entrepreneurial husbands. Tyler could invite his hipster English department friends and their skinny, chain-smoking wives. The house would have bay windows, a marble countertop kitchen, and a cozy little sunroom where you could curl up and read a magazine on a cold winter night with an afghan laid across your lap. A spacious house they could fill with two or three well-mannered yet playfully rambunctious children.

Anna was on good terms with the other cocktail waitresses, bartenders, blackjack dealers, and Lucky Coyote staff, but it was hard to have much of a conversation with them. They seemed as foggy as the clients they served, constantly checking their watches as they counted the minutes until their shift, or double shift, ended. Everyone wore forest green Lucky Coyote polo shirts and blue jeans. Sometimes the female members of the casino staff showed up with their hair still wet, complaining of defective alarm clocks while they looked around skittishly with dark-ringed eyes. The male staffers were forty or older, with ex-wives, rocky job histories, and permanent hangovers. They talked endlessly of sports, any sport, reeling off names Anna didn't know while analyzing the over and under for each game being played on American soil. She couldn't speak to them without their well-oiled eyes slipping to her chest, where they finally came into focus with an intensity they usually reserved for the lounge TVs.

One evening Anna left work and began the two-mile walk home. She walked along the edge of the highway, idly wondering if the usual truck full of leering rednecks would drive by and hoot at her. When she reached the first houses on the edge of town, the highway became Main Street and a sidewalk sprang up as if just for her. The sun had set, but the heat of the day held on in a dry simmer.

Anna skipped her turnoff and continued down Main Street, deciding to check in on Mr. Diaz and see how his vigil was going. It had been more than three weeks since the landing and the town was finally getting used to having the meteorite around. People gathered around the crater less often now (except the teenagers, who had nowhere better to hang out), and the mayor's resolutions to put up gift shops and charge admission had been tabled indefinitely. The Wormwood city council failed to imagine why anyone would want to drive two hours north of Las Vegas to see a small pit, a dark rock at the bottom of the pit, and a Mexican with a poster-board sign. How could that compete with the glitzy Vegas strip or the Hoover Dam? And who wanted a bunch of tourists waltzing through town anyway, raising dust and taking the good bar stools?

As Anna approached the parking lot, she found the area

empty except for Taco Thunder's owner. Bundled in a dirty white comforter, Mr. Diaz sat in his recliner inside a three-sided, bus-stop-like structure Rosa Diaz had commissioned to protect her husband from the elements. The windbreak was made out of wood, its interior padded with six inches of fiberglass insulation and a half-inch layer of Sheetrock. The windbreak's slanting roof overhung the shelter's opening a good three feet, providing additional shelter from sun and rain. Anna entered the wooden shelter and sat beside Mr. Diaz on one of the folding chairs. He'd lost weight, and his already tan skin had deepened in color, cracking with lines that hadn't been there before.

"Hello, Mr. Diaz. I don't know if you remember me, but I'm Anna Mayfield. Bernie Turner's niece." Mr. Diaz nodded. To their left, Taco Thunder was lit more brightly than the old Mr. Diaz would have found necessary. Anna noticed that a two-foot-high wire-mesh fence, the kind farmers used to keep hungry rabbits out of a vegetable patch, ringed the crater's edge.

"What's with the fence?"

"Animals," Mr. Diaz said. "They kept falling into the pit and dying."

Mr. Diaz shifted beneath his blanket. A dirty hand appeared and tapped the sign at his feet. Anna leaned closer.

"Ah. The end is near."

Mr. Diaz tucked the hand back under the comforter. Anna stuck her hands in her pockets. She felt the metal points of her house keys in one, the raised bumps of her cell phone's keypad in the other. The scent of cooked peppers and hamburger drifted over from Taco Thunder.

"So how near are we talking? I mean, is the world going to end tonight?"

Mr. Diaz sniffed the air. "I do not know."

"But sometime soon?"

"Yes. Soon."

Anna stood up and looked in the crater. The meteorite sat at the bottom of the pit, a lump of dense black nestled within the crater's general murk. Anna imagined a giant coming along and scooping up the meteorite for a souvenir. He'd whistle jauntily as he carried it away, hefting its dense weight in the palm of his hand.

Anna blinked and pulled back from the crater. She'd been leaning farther over the fence than she realized, her ankles pushing at the short fence until the sharp metal ends dug into her skin, almost drawing blood. Her neck hurt, too. How long had she been staring into the crater, exactly? The sky was definitely darker now, full-on nighttime. Anna sat back down.

"I have these dreams. About the end of the world."

Mr. Diaz shifted in his chair.

"Every dream, or I guess nightmare, is different. Nuclear war. Plagues. Earthquakes. Super tsunamis that wash everything away. They feel pretty real, too. I wake up sweaty and my whole body shakes."

"You have these dreams often?"

"Every night." Anna tucked her hair behind her ears.

"What do you think they mean? I mean, locusts? I had one about locusts eating through brick walls. Freaking locusts."

"The manner of the end itself doesn't matter, Mrs. Mayfield. Via nature, God, or man, the end is near. You should be sitting beside me, telling people their time upon this world is perilously short."

Anna smirked, imagining herself wrapped in a second dirty white comforter. Tyler could bring her paper bags full of candy bars and thermoses filled with hot soup while she held up a sign of her own, shouting prophesies laced with spittle.

"Your heart grows faint. The end of the world is not a popularity contest, Mrs. Mayfield. Do you think I've chosen to sit here day after day because I like having my words mocked by others? That I sit here because I enjoy it when asshole teenagers toss eggs at me and wrap my sleeping form in toilet paper?"

Anna stood up. "No, I'm sorry. I'm not ready for that level of action just yet. They're just nightmares."

"And I'm just crazy."

"Probably."

Mr. Diaz surprised her by smiling, revealing a crooked set of teeth. "I hope so, Mrs. Mayfield. I'd much prefer madness to the destruction of everything I have ever known, or loved. I hope it is that simple."

Anna took a tube of lip gloss out of her pocket and moistened her lips. All this dry air and wind chapped her skin and frizzed her hair. It was terrible. No wonder half the people in town looked like they'd been carved out of wood. You had to moisturize constantly, just to stay even.

Tyler watched Anna undress later that night in their bedroom. After the many years of sex and general nudity, Anna didn't see what was so exotic about her naked body, not to mention the lingering casino smell of menthol cigarettes, peppermint chewing gum, and undercooked prime rib that clung to her at night, even if she changed out of her work clothes. Tyler lay on his side while he watched her, propped up on his elbow with a hand beneath his cheek.

Anna took off her bra and fingered the red lines it left on her skin. She could feel his eyes on her, and she knew he was imagining touching her like that himself. She lingered in her inspection.

"You're so beautiful."

"I am?"

"You don't even know how beautiful."

"We've just been stuck in Wormwood too long. You've forgotten all the options out there."

"I know a hottie when I see one."

"Sure you do."

Anna rubbed the stretch marks on her hips. They'd showed up out of nowhere when she was only twelve. She hadn't known she was supposed to rub cocoa butter into her skin to prevent the wavy white lines. She hadn't known squat.

"I bet you could enter Miss America tomorrow and win the whole shebang."

Anna turned and jutted out a hip. "Now you're just trying to get laid, Mr. Mayfield."

"I'm serious. You'd win like crazy. The other girls would cry."

"Twenty-seven might as well be fifty in that contest. Besides, I bet the game's changed. Teenagers getting their ass and tits lifted. And I'm not getting my lips injected with that collagen crap. No thank you."

Anna slid into bed. Tyler reached across her and turned off the light. He pushed a button on the clock to set the alarm. Anna turned toward him as he ran a hand down her hip. His touch was always so soft, as if he was afraid of setting off a bomb.

"I chatted with Mr. Diaz on my way home."

"Yeah?"

"The Meteor is still coming."

"I hope not. I don't want my last days on earth to be spent teaching summer school." Tyler kissed her shoulder and ran his lips up her neck. Anna kissed him and turned onto her side.

"I'm sorry, Ty. I'm too tired."

Tyler cupped her right breast and squeezed it. "Is it okay if I hump your leg for a minute?"

Anna nuzzled her pillow and adjusted it beneath her head. "Knock yourself out. Humping is your marital right."

Tyler gave a few dry thrusts, but stopped when she didn't

laugh. He released her breast and rolled over. A few minutes later, his breathing slowed and he started to snore. Anna felt exhaustion pull at her. She thought about Mr. Diaz, sitting across town in his recliner in the cold desert night, surviving on the food and water his family brought to him and using the restaurant's bathroom when nature called. She wondered how well he slept these days.

FIFTEEN

Wormwood's population waited indoors for the sun to go down, drinking cold beer and lemonade while they listened to their air conditioners rattle and watched TV. It was the Fourth of July. The wind whipped through town all afternoon, throwing sand and harassing the flowerbeds. Bernie told Tyler it had been ten years since they'd held a parade downtown in the summer heat and it wasn't missed much, not even by the children. They played cribbage in the dining room while they waited for Anna to come home from the casino. When she finally showed up at dusk, Bernie heated hot dogs in the microwave and they ate their Fourth of July dinner at the dining room table, with cold air blowing down the back of their necks.

After dinner was over, Bernie threw a chilled six-pack of beer into a canvas bag. Anna changed out of her work clothes, and Tyler got three collapsible camping chairs out of the garage. They headed west through town, with Roscoe leading the way, and it was nearly dark by the time they got to the fireworks' site, a clearing of sand and sagebrush that gave a beautiful view of the mountain range. The mountains were old and worn down, nothing more than a series of looping curves set against the lighter blue-black darkness of the sky. Hundreds of people had already shown up at the site and claimed their territory, throwing square islands of tarp and blanket on top of the sand. Charcoal grills had been rolled in, and the smells of roasting bratwurst, hamburger, and sweet corn swirled above the crowd.

They passed through the crowd until they found an open spot. Anna laid out the blanket and Tyler set up the camping chairs. Tyler's chair was narrow and pressed against his hips. He took off his sandals and dug his toes into the blanket, feeling the stored warmth rising up from the sand below. Lights came on in the crowd as families turned on their electric camping lanterns. Minor fireworks popped in the distance as amateurs grew impatient for the featured presentation. Someone was handing out lit sparklers and children ran with them through the crowd, holding the sparklers above their heads like magic wands. Tyler saw Merritt Jackson riding through the crowd, Sadie's head swaying from side to side as the horse sniffed for treats.

A fizzy patch of green fireworks bloomed and faded in the north. His brother had loved fireworks. Loved them. For the first few months after Cody's disappearance, Tyler's mother had stayed in bed. She didn't cook, she didn't clean, she didn't go in to her part-time job at the bank. She just lay in bed with a pillow over her face. Tyler would sit with his mother after school and wonder if she was dying. Sometimes he would crawl into bed with her, even though he was twelve and too old for stuff like that. He'd put a pillow over his own face and fall asleep. When Tyler's father came home from work in the evening, he'd find his wife and remaining son lying together in complete silence, like unconscious survivors floating on a raft. His father would do his best to be loud and upbeat. He'd make them spaghetti, or grill steaks, and they'd eat dinner together in the kitchen as if everything were normal, and no one would mention how wild his mother's hair was, how it had snarled and knotted like a homeless woman's.

Anna set her hand on his shoulder. "What are you thinking about, Ty?"

"Nothing. Just waiting for the show."

"You looked sad."

"I'm okay."

"It's your brother, isn't it? You were thinking about Cody."

Tyler shrugged and drank his beer. Anna scooted her chair closer to his and set her head on his shoulder. The tip of his aunt's cigarette burned like a miniature sun as she smoked. Another amateur firework popped in the distance and the crowd rustled, getting restless. "Show should start any minute now," Bernie said. "They like to wait until it gets pitch-black. The city workers here are serious about their fireworks."

The last sparkler fizzled down and kids were called back to their blanket islands. The electric lanterns were switched off as the crowd hushed. A puffed explosion sounded in the distance, as if cued by the crowd's silence, and a shadowy ball rose whistling into the air. It detonated high above the mountain line in a burst of gold and the boom of its report echoed off the mountains. The crowd cheered and leaned back in their seats.

The fireworks were good, but Tyler found his eyes dropping to the crowd and watching the colors change against their skin and clothes. He liked the kaleidoscopic effect the fireworks had. The crowd turned gold. Orange. Green.

Tyler noticed a child in the crowd with his back turned to the fireworks show, watching him.

No.

Not a child.

The gray man. The space alien.

Tyler sat up in his chair, but didn't stand. Last time, the alien had disappeared before he could talk to it. He needed to let it make the first move, to approach him on its own terms. Holy shit. That was an alien out there in the crowd, watching him. He hadn't even smoked any pot this time and there it was, staring.

The sky and the crowd went dark. This was the pause before the grand finale, the final five minutes of shock and awe. Tyler shook Anna's shoulder.

"Honey."

"What?"

"Watch the crowd."

"What?"

"When the fireworks start again. Watch the crowd."

"Why?"

"You'll see."

Three thumping shots and the finale began, filaments of red, white, and blue screaming across the sky, clawing at the smoke. Tyler scanned the crowd but couldn't find the alien again. It had disappeared. It had nothing to say tonight, and maybe nothing to say to Tyler, period. What was there to talk about, anyway? What would an alien want with him? The whole thing was ridiculous. He was having a nervous breakdown, dealing with those summer school kids. They didn't want to learn about composition. They wanted to live on the Internet, sleep on their desktops, and get wasted after their parents went to bed. He wasn't teaching. He was herding the last generation of drooling humanity through the gates until they reached the slaughterhouse of environmental destruction.

"Wow," Anna said. "You're right, Ty."

Tyler sat up and scanned the crowd again. He couldn't find the rounded gray head, the almond-shaped eyes. The crowd was watching the sky change colors with each detonation. Anna set her hand on his knee.

"Everyone looks so happy right now, don't they? Turning all those colors."

"Yeah," Tyler said. "I thought you might want to see that."

The crowd left the fireworks show in a steadily walking mass, carrying their chairs, blankets, and coolers. Tyler had the collapsible chairs slung over his shoulder in their nylon bags, and they whacked against his back with each step. Roscoe pulled at his leash, straining toward all the running children as they passed by giggling. Anna and Bernie were talking about Betsy Ross and the original American flag, but Tyler couldn't follow the conversation because it was too boring. Someone had a radio and was playing the Charlie Daniels Band loud enough for everyone to hear. You could tell who was drunk and who wasn't by how much they slanted as they walked. One woman ahead of them slanted so much she fell over laughing into the sand. Her husband grabbed her hands and pulled the woman to her feet. She laughed some more. He ran his hands down her arms, chest, and legs, brushing off the sand as he drunkenly scolded her.

They reached the edge of town. Almost every front-porch light was on. Tyler fell behind the others and scrutinized the shadows in each yard they passed. The alien could be anywhere, watching him. The alien could be following him right now, waiting for him to fall asleep before silently appearing at the foot of his bed, those enormous, ageless eyes watching him sleep beside his wife.

Outside the house, Bernie hung back as Anna went inside.

"Ty."

"Yes, ma'am?"

"You look spooked."

"I'm fine, Aunt Bernie. Don't worry about me."

"No, you're not. You're spooked. I know when a man is spooked, and tonight that's you. It's nothing to be ashamed of."

"I think I saw a space alien. At the fireworks show."

Bernie latched the gate and pulled at it to make sure it was secure. In the dark, she looked a lot like his mother, closing her own gate back in Omaha. All these women, Tyler thought. Latching all these gates.

"Are you sure it was an alien?"

"Pretty sure. It's the second time I've seen it. I saw it in your backyard, too. Right after the meteorite landed."

Bernie rubbed the back of her neck as she peered up at him. She was quiet for a long time. "Tyler," she said, "there's some folks I think you should meet."

SIXTEEN

July swept through Wormwood like a red plague. Inside the bubble of heat, blowing sand, and the rattle of air-conditioning pushed to its limits, Anna's nightmares continued. She shouted herself awake in the middle of the night, delirious and slapping at the air. By the time morning finally came around, she and Tyler would groggily lie in bed together, motionless and exhausted. She no longer relayed her nightmares to Tyler aloud, but each morning she'd take his hand and squeeze it in a way that somehow conveyed the terror she'd gone through yet again. They spent their weekends wandering around town in a daze, talking about their jobs and going on vacations they couldn't afford and friends far away.

Anna started staying up late to watch TV with Roscoe after everyone else had gone to bed. The dog slept curled on top of her feet, snoring softly while Anna flicked through cable programming and ate reduced-fat microwave popcorn.

One Friday night, she fell asleep during a talk show and woke up to find herself alone in the living room. She brushed the popcorn crumbs off the front of her shirt and collapsed the recliner's footrest. "Roscoe?"

The house was quiet. Anna went into the kitchen, but Roscoe wasn't at his water dish, or pawing at the cupboard where Bernie kept his chew bones. Anna checked Bernie's room, but the door was closed, and she never let Roscoe sleep in her bedroom, anyway. The air-conditioning was on, but the house was warmer than usual. Anna went back to the living room and noticed hot air coming from the front hall. The outer door was open. Anna padded barefoot through the hallway and stepped out onto the front steps. It was a warm night, with cloudless skies and a full moon that had turned the entire town chalk white. Anna called for Roscoe, but the bushes didn't rustle and the dog didn't appear. The fence gate lay open to the street.

Anna put on a bra and sandals and went out. She took a flashlight with her, a heavy Maglite, and kept its beam tracing the sidewalk in front of her. The air smelled baked and wet at the same time, the nighttime sprinklers in full effect as they doused the town's patchy, desperate lawns. Nearly every house's interior was dark, and the few lights she did see came from attic windows, where the shades were drawn. She headed downtown, walking quickly. She didn't shout for the dog.

From a distance, Mr. Diaz didn't look any different than he normally did. He sat in his recliner, rocking gently and bundled in his comforter. He was quiet, staring across the meteor crater as if he could see through the buildings around him and millions of miles distant, into the dark pockets of space. It was only as Anna drew closer to the meteorite crater that she noticed something was wrapped around his mouth. Some kind of silver fabric . . . no, duct tape, and it was wrapped around his chest, too, in several layers, binding him to the recliner. And he wasn't rocking; he was trying to get loose.

Anna clicked off the flashlight. She heard whispering coming from the crater. Sounds of struggle. What the hell? She crossed the parking lot carefully, stepping over the bigger chunks of asphalt and trying not to make any noise. Mr. Diaz saw her and began murmuring louder through the duct tape, trying to nod his head. Anna waved her flashlight and leaned over to look.

On the crater floor, four teenage boys struggled with something big. At first it looked like another boy, flailing his limbs, but when the boys fell back for a second, repulsed, Anna caught a glimpse of a white-fur-covered stomach and realized it was Roscoe. The dog had duct tape around its muzzle, so it could only growl from the back of its throat, and they'd pinned him against the meteorite on his back. The dog thrashed against the boys' grasp, trying to right himself, and the boys swore quietly as they tried to keep him pinned.

One of the boys—he couldn't have been older than fourteen—reached down, picked something off the ground, and lifted it above his head. It was a butcher's knife, and its steel blade shone in the moonlight. Anna felt the blood rise in her cheeks. Even as a little girl, she'd hated boys who did things like this. The boys who tortured frogs and set chickens on fire to watch them run. Hurting defenseless creatures for fun was as low as a human being got.

"What the fuck do you think you're doing?"

The boy lowered the knife and took a step backward. The other boys released the dog and turned to look up at Anna. Anna clicked on the flashlight and shined its beam in their eyes.

"You goddamn little pukes. You were about to kill that poor dog, weren't you?"

Roscoe scrabbled at the air, turned over, and dropped to the crater floor. He torpedoed one of the boys in the crotch with his snout and knocked him to the ground. The two other boys looked from their fallen comrade to the boy with the knife. He sneered into the light. "Don't worry. It's just some lady."

The fallen boy wrestled with Roscoe, who couldn't bite with the tape around his jaws, and the boy got clear long enough to jump up and start climbing out of the crater. The other boys followed him, scrambling fast, while the boy with the knife jumped on top of the meteorite, out of the dog's reach. The boy pointed the knife toward Anna.

"You interrupted us. You interrupted the sacrifice."

"Come up here. We're going to visit your mother."

"The meteorite wants blood."

"I don't think so."

"Maybe it wants your blood."

"C'mon. Drop that knife and get your ass up here."

The boy picked his teeth with the tip of the knife. His teeth looked terrible, as if their crowns had been broken and shoved inward. Crystal meth did that. Anna had seen commercials. He was a meth head.

"Go away," the boy said. "We don't need a fucking little woman getting in the way."

Anna turned, dropped her arm, and brought it around again as she hurled the flashlight as hard as she could. It struck the boy in the chest and Anna jumped in after it, landing on top of the boy and knocking his skinny butt to the ground. The flashlight had punched the wind out of him and Anna was able to take the knife away easily while he gasped and struggled, butting his head against her chest. Anna slapped the boy down and got to her feet. Roscoe nosed Anna's crotch in greeting, almost knocking her off balance. She ran a hand through the dog's fur, feeling for any wounds. The flashlight was still shining and it lay on the ground, illuminating the crater. The boy stopped writhing and sat up, blood streaming from his nose. Anna looked down and saw that her shirt was soaked with the same blood.

"Jesus," she gasped. "What a mess."

Anna let the meth boy slink off with his bloody nose and a warning to leave helpless animals alone if he wanted to keep his testicles in the future. She cut Mr. Diaz free from the duct tape and together they lifted Roscoe out of the crater. Anna ripped the gray tape off Roscoe's snout and the dog submitted to the pain bravely, licking his chops when it was over. "You see," Mr. Diaz said, scratching the dog behind the ears, "this world needs to be cleansed."

"Maybe," Anna said, "but that's enough action for me tonight."

The house was still asleep when Anna and Roscoe returned. Shaking with adrenaline, Anna went into the kitchen and took off her bloody T-shirt. Roscoe nabbed the shirt from her hand and raced around the living room, happy with his new prize. Anna let him run while she dug under the sink, pulling out a plastic garbage bag. The blood was all down her front now. She unzipped her jeans and dropped them in the bag. She took off her bra and panties and stuffed them in the bag, too. Totally naked now, she walked back into the living room and pried her shirt from Roscoe, who seemed genuinely disappointed to have his new bloody toy taken away.

Anna gave the dog an extra treat, shoved the shirt to the bottom of the kitchen trash, and went upstairs. She was glad Bernie hadn't woken up to see her nude and streaked with blood. How could she have explained that? She'd been abducted by aliens, forced to kill another abductee, and had just escaped from the mothership? Ha. Bernie would love that one. And the whole thing was insane, anyway. The kids had learned their lesson and she was new in town, an easy target for gossip, good or bad. Unless more pets started disappearing, she might as well keep the whole ordeal between her, Mr. Diaz, and the dog.

She found Tyler buried under pillows in their bedroom, snoring and sprawled in the middle of the bed. Anna went into the bathroom without turning on a light. She didn't want to see herself in the mirror. No need to see the war paint reflected; she could see it for herself when she looked down. The pipes rattled to life as she ran the bath. When the water was warm enough, she flipped the shower lever and stepped into the tub. The hot water stung her cold cheeks and chest. She found the bar of soap in the dark and rubbed it down her front. When she was certain she'd washed off most of the blood, she slipped her arm past the shower curtain and flipped on the light switch. A few patches of coppery red had dried on her stomach. Anna rubbed at them with her thumb and felt the last tremors of energy wash through her body, heightening her senses.

SEVENTEEN

Bernie drove Tyler across town to a compact, purple house. His aunt still hadn't told Tyler whom he was going to meet, and he wasn't sure he really wanted to know. They went up the front walk and Bernie knocked on the door. A middle-aged man with brown, curly hair answered the door, smiling. His pink face glowed, as if freshly scrubbed, and he was dressed in a spotless navy blue suit and a red tie. He had enormous aquamarine eyes.

"Hey, Felix. This is my nephew, Tyler Mayfield."

Felix took Tyler's hand and shook it, still smiling. "Good evening, Tyler. I'm Felix Hill. We're so glad you could make it tonight."

Felix stepped back and ushered them inside. The house was cold. They went through an entryway and stepped into a living room. Several mismatched armchairs filled the space and had been pulled into a circle around a coffee table. On the table was a paper plate filled with brownies, a silver carafe of coffee, and several white porcelain cups. A man in blue jeans and a Nascar T-shirt sat talking to a thin, finely boned woman with silver hair. The man and the woman looked up as they entered the room. Felix Hill stopped and clasped his hands behind his back.

"My friends, the guest of the hour has arrived. Lila Fanon and Ray Boones, this is Bernie's nephew, Tyler Mayfield."

For a second, Tyler thought they might clap. They got to their feet instead and came over to shake his hand, their feet skimming across the floor in their hurry to introduce themselves. Hands were shaken all around. Somebody put a cup of coffee into Tyler's hand and a brownie into the other. He found himself sinking into an armchair covered in cobalt blue crushed velour. The group sat down around him, grinning as they sipped their coffee.

"You must not get a lot of visitors here."

The room burst out laughing, like this was the most hysterical thing they'd ever heard. Their heads flew back, jaws opened wide. He could see a lot of silver fillings. Tyler looked into his cup and wished he was drinking something stronger than coffee.

"Please forgive us," Felix Hill said, once the laughter receded, "but you've hit on a particularly acute funny bone among us. You see, Tyler, your lovely aunt has brought you to a meeting of the Wormwood Visitation Society, and the term 'visitors' holds a different meaning for us than it does to your average Joe on the street.

"To fully understand my meaning, I must tell you a story

about what happened to me five years ago. Quite the bachelor, I was living in Denver and working as a lawyer. One day, I learned my father, who I loved very much, had passed away from a heart attack across town. The night after his funeral, I drank a glass of Scotch, took a bath, and went to bed early. Several hours passed and still I couldn't sleep, so I stared at the ceiling and counted backward from one thousand. Around seven hundred, I began to float above my own body. Truly. I floated through the roof of my home as if the particles of my body had been turned into air. I flew high above the earth, across the atmosphere layers, and into outer space. I soared across the universe, stars blurring around me. When my solar flight ended, I was standing on another planet.

"I was on a high mountain peak. The view was absolutely astounding. I had never seen anything so beautiful and lush. The sun was a pale, pale yellow and the sky was opal blue. The air was cool, but not cold. The ground below was a green plain as far as the horizon, spotted with all sorts of colorful dots that I took for alpine wildflowers. Huge, shaggy creatures lumbered across the fields, as immense as woolly mammoths, but moving with such orderly assurance one could assume a high degree of intelligence.

"The drop to the grassy fields below must have gone on for miles. I was wondering how I was going to descend without the assistance of climbing gear when a warm voice spoke inside my head and assured me that I wasn't dreaming. The voice told me my soul had flown across the astral plane and landed on this new, distant world. The voice also informed me that I, among all the inhabitants of earth, had been chosen to first receive their offering of friendship."

Felix paused and took a white silk handkerchief from his suit coat's breast pocket. He was sweating despite the air-conditioning.

"What I was told then, Tyler, was the best possible news you could hope to hear in these positively hellish times of strife, pain, and despair."

Tyler set his coffee cup down on the table. "What? What did they say?"

Felix Hill smiled and gazed at the ceiling.

"They're coming. Yes, sir. They're already on their way."

Felix waited for the others to stop applauding before he continued. "Don't be alarmed. This race, whom we refer to as the Visitors, wish us nothing but good. They simply want to apply their vast knowledge, resources, and technical capacity to the problems of our world in hopes of easing us into the next evolutionary phase of our existence. A phase that doesn't involve war, hunger, and disease. They want to help us, and in return they only ask our friendship, respect, and love. Could you ask for a better deal than that? No. I don't think so."

Felix dabbed more sweat off his forehead. "That fateful night of my father's funeral, the Visitors appointed me the task of moving to central Nevada and creating a group of open-minded souls to ease the transitional pains of their arrival. A welcome group of sorts that could act as mediator between the earthly authorities and the Visitors. The good people in this room have joined with me in preparing this welcome committee, and now, Tyler, we'd like you to join us, also."

Tyler glanced around the room. "You want me to join?"

"Nothing would make us happier."

"Me?"

"Your aunt tells me you've been having visions since you arrived in town. Visions of an alien being?"

"You think they're related to the Visitors?"

"They may be. And you saw the meteor land, didn't you? Truly, could there have been a more obvious portent than that?"

Tyler stuffed the rest of his brownie into his mouth and chewed. The room was quiet while they waited for him to finish chewing. Felix Hill peered down at him from behind steepled fingers

"Ty, I totally understand your hesitancy. This task, if you choose to help us undertake it, won't be an easy one. When they arrive, it's going to be a shock. Real live aliens, landing on earth. Landing in Nevada, U.S.A. The Russians won't like it. The Germans won't like it. And the Chinese definitely, definitely won't like it. War may be threatened. Fingers will dally above buttons, itching to obliterate this entire planet in fiery orange waves.

"That's where the Wormwood Visitation Society will come in. Working out of this very house, we'll act as a buffer between the Visitors and the authorities. We'll translate, somehow. We'll interpret. Soothing as a cold washcloth against a child's feverish forehead, we'll make certain everyone remains calm and ensure that the nations of the world 'chill out' and play nice with the Visitors. But until that fateful day, as far as the general population is concerned, the W.V.S. is simply an amateur astronomy club that meets once a week to talk about the wonders of outer space."

Bernie coughed into her fist and smiled at her nephew. Tyler wiped his hands on the front of his shorts.

"But why here? If the aliens want publicity, why land in central Nevada? Why not land in New York, or L.A.?"

"That's a wonderful question," Felix said, nodding. "I've considered that question myself, and I have determined that such dense, overpopulated environments, while providing high levels of exposure, are highly unstable due to the complexity of their inner workings. The Visitors have no wish to upset great pockets of the human population, but simply wish to spread the word of their arrival and show humanity that they come with only peace and love in their hearts. You show up in New York City unannounced and everyone is immediately thinking 'Oh jeez, *War of the Worlds*.' Women scream and run through the streets with their children in their arms. Men retrieve pistols from glove compartments and start waving them about wildly. In the ensuing chaos, the United States believes it is under attack and responds with maximum, perhaps even nuclear, force. How much easier, and simpler, to arrive gently, in a town of three thousand souls, on a warm summer night. How fantastically sedate."

Tyler rubbed his face with his hands. He wanted to laugh, get to his feet, and run screaming from the room, but the image of the gray, dark-eyed being kept popping into his mind, boring through him with those primordial eyes. And that second appearance, during the fireworks.

"Sure," Tyler said, looking at his aunt. "Why not?"

Tyler had Bernie drop him off downtown after the society meeting and joined Clyde Ringston and Merritt Jackson at the bar. Tyler drank whiskey and Cokes and ate stale, oversalted popcorn. Merritt and Clyde were talking about the Texas Rangers for some reason and Merritt kept bringing up Nolan Ryan, again and again and again. The sheriff was drinking straight bourbon. "Radar Love" played on the jukebox and Tyler mindlessly nodded along to the music. "Arleen's got a new Silverton boyfriend," Clyde announced. "He's a mortgage banker."

"A mortgage banker?"

"He's in a cover band. They play a lot of Fleetwood Mac."

Merritt grunted and shook his head. "Good Lord. I bet he wears fancy Italian cologne, too."

"She says she's going to file for divorce. What's twenty-five years of marriage, anyhow?"

Tyler licked his lips and turned around. He inspected the face of every man in the bar. Find Cody. Find Cody.

"Ty?"

He swiveled around on his stool. Tracy smiled at him from behind the bar.

"Yes, ma'am?"

"You're empty. You need another drink?"

"How about a beer? And a glass of ice water."

"Sure thing."

The men watched as Tracy fixed a glass of ice water and took a bottle of beer out of the cooler. She set the drinks in front of Tyler and went back to the other end of the bar, where a woman was waving to get her attention. Her chestnut hair caught the dim bar lights and glowed, as if each strand was lit from within.

Clyde whistled softly and hung his head. Tyler clapped him on the shoulder.

"Clyde, Clyde, Clyde. What you should do is get a hobby."

"A hobby?"

"You know. Something to distract you."

"I could try Russian roulette."

"Yeah," Tyler said. "Or maybe something that doesn't involve blowing off your head. You could become a rock collector."

"A rock collector?"

Tyler slammed his glass on the table. "Gentlemen, did you know this entire town is now considered a strewn field? Little pieces of meteorite could be sitting out in the desert right now as we speak, waiting for a savvy rock hunter to find them. Sure, the main meteor landed in Taco Thunder's parking lot, but that doesn't mean smaller pieces didn't break off during its descent. And do you know what meteorite fragments can fetch at auction?"

"No."

"A ton. Thousands. Sometimes millions."

"You're kidding me."

"You never know what someone will buy," Merritt said, sipping his bourbon. "A fool and his money."

"So what do you do? Just start walking around and hope you see one?"

"I don't know," Tyler said. "You probably want to take some sort of handbook to make sure you can tell the difference between meteorites and regular rocks. And a map. To show you where you've been already."

Tracy came back down the bar and poured a beer from the tap. The jukebox changed to "Brown Sugar." The bartender's curved hips swayed to the music, as if she was about to hop across the bar and hit the dance floor. Clyde finished his drink.

"Strewn field, huh?"

Tyler took the long way home, swaying down the sidewalks of Wormwood and studying each home like a drunken building inspector. He'd left the bar before last call, but not by much. Merritt and Clyde had started talking about baseball again and that was enough of that. He needed to find some friends who liked to read a book once in a while, not just westerns and insurance policies. Hopefully, he'd meet somebody when the high school teachers came back for the fall semester. He'd make friends with everybody. He'd invite all the teachers over to Bernie's and grill hot dogs, barbecue chicken, and veggie burgers. They could call it a "Welcome to Wormwood" party. He could invite his parents to visit from Omaha. Hire a DJ. They'd get a keg and plastic cups for everyone.

Tyler turned down another street. He didn't recognize this one, and the lighting wasn't anything to write home about, either. Only one lamp, and it was at the end of the street. Dead end.

"Turn back, ye who enter here."

Tyler grinned at his own joke. He turned around to take his own advice and caught a blur of movement in the corner of his eye. He dropped into a crouch, expecting to see the space alien, but the street was empty except for a single parked car, a rusty boat of an Oldsmobile. The movement had come from the car. Two shapes struggled in the rear window. The palm of someone's hand slapped at the glass and Tyler, alarmed, lurched forward to check things out.

The Oldsmobile's windows were open to the warm night. He could hear moaning, but no screaming. The victim might have been gagged already, or had a knife to her throat. Tyler came up beside the driver side rear window and peered inside. It was hard to make out the two figures in the dim light, but he saw a lot of white flesh, dark hair, and glinting flecks of metal. A pale breast, exposed to the air. Two faces, oblivious of him and locked together at the mouth.

Tyler fell back from the window. He reexamined the Oldsmobile, finally recognizing it from the high school parking lot. This was Skull's car. That was Skull and his girlfriend in there, having car sex. No one was being raped or violently assaulted with a tire iron. Just two sweaty teenagers doing what teenagers did on a Saturday night.

"Sorry. Sorry." Tyler strode away from the car and headed in what he hoped was the general direction of his aunt's house. His face burned. He wanted the lights of Wormwood so far behind him they seemed like nothing but haloed specks in his vision. He wanted the amnesia of the desert.

EIGHTEEN

Anna floated through the rest of July and into August, unable to grab her thoughts and put them in any useful order. She was too tired. The apocalyptic nightmares absorbed her energy, and the time she spent sleeping was more exhausting than the time she spent awake. She couldn't call it insomnia, because she slept, if fitfully, and she couldn't call it a nervous breakdown, because she managed to go to work, eat three square meals, and go on walks with her husband in the evening. Anna didn't know what to call it. Something like this had never happened to her before. She wasn't the kind of person who had nightmares about the end of the world. She dreamt about stupid crap, like torn stockings or gaining thirty pounds overnight and having a job interview the next day. Those were her types of nightmares.

Whenever Tyler and Bernie left for one of their astronomy club meetings, Anna scrolled through her cell phone's contact list to find someone from back home to call. Each time, she set aside the phone and called no one. She read children's books. She bought a dream journal and filled its pages with unreadable scribbles and spiraling doodles, specializing in chunky, bricklike monsters with gaping mouths and triangular monster teeth. Sometimes Anna sketched people and fuzzy animals running away from the monsters, and sometimes the monsters were on fire, flames engulfing their chunky bodies. She burned incense. She took long showers, running the water until it grew cold and her skin was tinted blue. She cut caffeine out of her diet, drank nothing but herbal tea and water. She visited Wormwood Methodist two Sundays in a row. She sat in the back row and emptied her thoughts and listened to the service as if it were a thousand miles away, carried to her ears by satellite radio, and afterward Anna mingled with the other worshippers and engaged in bright, meaningless conversations that tasted like muskmelon on her tongue. She wore makeup every day, and didn't leave the house until she was satisfied with her appearance. She tried every coping mechanism she knew. The world kept ending.

Anna drove downtown to get groceries one Tuesday, her mind foggy and burnt, as usual. The sky was overcast for the first time in weeks. Children played on front lawns, dousing one another with squirt guns and hurling themselves down water-slicked tarps. Anna imagined them all growing up as meth heads, as potential sacrificial killers.

The grocery store was well stocked, with fourteen aisles of

merchandise and slick waxed floors. Anna grabbed a cart and started down the first aisle, in no particular hurry. She enjoyed the air-conditioning, the nonsmoking atmosphere, even the bouncy Muzak.

Anna turned down aisle 2. Two men in black suits and dark sunglasses stood talking to an old lady near the end of the aisle. Clean shaved, they had skinny black ties and square, broad shoulders. One man stood in front of the old lady's grocery cart, blocking her way. Anna drew back out of sight. Feds, of course. G-men. They couldn't have looked any more conspicuous in Wormwood if they'd tried. They spoke in low, deep voices, but the old lady couldn't understand them and made them speak louder, until their voices rumbled with annoyance.

"We just need to know if you've seen anything suspicious."

"What's suspicious?"

"Strange behavior, ma'am. Have you seen any prowlers in your neighborhood recently? Anyone you didn't recognize?"

"They egged my house last Halloween. It was horrible. They got the toilet paper stuck in my rosebushes and it was the cheap kind, the one-ply. It pulls apart as soon as you touch it. Just shreds in your hand."

"What about recently, ma'am? Have you had any prowlers recently?"

"I don't think so."

"Has anyone broken into your garage? Shed?"

"No."

"What about pets? Have you lost any pets?"

Anna pushed her cart on. She'd heard enough. She could tell the Feds all about strange behavior and missing pets, but the agents flat out gave her the creeps. What was with the sunglasses? Why did they hide their eyes? And their voices— they sounded like violent men barely in control of themselves. Hard, self-righteous men. She wasn't too excited about the idea of getting into a car with them and being debriefed in some dark basement somewhere. What a creepy fucking idea. No. They could track down the stupid meth kids themselves. They had guns and suits and satellite imagery. They didn't need her help.

She propelled her cart through the dairy section, pausing just long enough to get cheese, yogurt, and milk. She turned down aisle 12, snagged some beer and a loaf of bread, and kept the cart rolling, wheels swiveling back and fourth, as if pulled in opposite directions. They'd be done interviewing the old lady by now. Surely they'd run into someone else to question before they noticed her leaving the store. The checkout girl, Naomi, was twirling her long red hair around her finger and reading a tabloid. Anna parked the cart in front of the checkout and unloaded it as fast as she could. Naomi smiled at Anna, shut the magazine, and set it back on the rack in front of the register. The tabloid's cover had a spaceman on it dressed in a flowing white robe.

ALIEN CRASHES IN UTAH: IMMEDIATELY CONVERTS TO MORMONISIM

Anna looked over her shoulder. She couldn't see the Feds, but that didn't mean they weren't coming.

Naomi ran everything over the scanner, bagging each item as it came. The computer totaled the cost, and Anna handed over her credit card.

"Weird, isn't it?"

Anna's head swiveled. "What?"

"That alien landing in Utah and turning all Mormon. That can't be real."

"No," Anna said, "it's probably not."

The credit card slip printed out, finally, and Naomi handed it over. Anna scribbled on the slip and handed it back. Naomi handed her two heavy plastic bags in return and tapped the tabloid's cover with a purple lacquered fingernail. "I can't believe they can print that sort of thing in the paper. That's lying, isn't it? They should be in jail for stuff like that."

"Totally," Anna said. "Thanks." She headed for the exit door. She could see two dark blurs on the edge of her vision, moving toward her. She kept her eyes on the exit and exhaled as the door slid open for her. A stiff wind was blowing, spraying sand against the grocery store and into Anna's face. She unlocked the Volvo's driver-side door and ducked inside, almost hitting her head on the roof. She dropped the plastic bags in the passenger seat and started the car. The two men in dark suits stepped out of the grocery store's exit. Anna reversed the car, trying not to push the accelerator too hard and spin her tires in an obviously guilty way. As she backed into the street she could see the Feds in the rearview mirror, standing beneath the stores faded awning, arms crossed as they watched her go. She laughed aloud and put a hand over her pounding heart. She'd gotten away.

NINETEEN

They headed to the fall site first thing in the morning, before it got too hot. The blue August sky was filled with hulking cumulus clouds that reminded Tyler of the blimps that flew above Memorial Stadium during Cornhusker games. As the clouds drifted slowly beneath the strong Nevada sun they threw enormous, cooling shadows on the ground. Tyler walked at the back of the group, watching his students talk to one another, their voices like the drone of bees. Today was the last day of class. Three of his students had dropped out within the first two weeks to face their grim futures alone, with poor composition skills, and the remaining seven had grown into a functioning, tightly knit unit through their shared boredom, apathy, and general malaise.

They reached the fall site in about fifteen minutes. Tyler had hoped the walk would take longer, but there you had it. Wormwood was not a big town.

Tyler gathered everyone in a group ten yards from the

crater. "Okay," he said. "Here we are. I know you've all been here before, but this time I want you to look at it through the eyes of a reporter. Or a poet. Or a novelist. Whatever. I just want you to gather enough information so you can write about it when we get back to school. We're going to spend all day on this assignment. It'll be twenty percent of your final grade."

The group shifted on their feet, already looking around for a place to sit. Skull raised his hand.

"Yes, Skull?"

"We can write what we want, as long as it has to do with the meteorite?"

"That's correct."

"Can we write about other stuff, too?"

"I'd like it to be centered on the meteorite, but you can go off track if you feel the piece calls for it."

The group broke up and scattered among the numerous folding chairs ringing the crater. They wrote in their note-books, heads bowed as they worked. Tyler joined Mr. and Mrs. Diaz beneath the shade of the Diaz's wooden shelter to watch the students work. The white comforter Mr. Diaz kept constantly wrapped around himself had turned gray with dirt and sweat, and he smelled terrible, but his eyes were as clear and focused as they'd been at the beginning of the summer, when he'd dragged his brown recliner across town and set it beside the crater.

"You have good students," Rosa said. "They look very studious."

"Maybe it's the meteorite. Maybe it has magical focusing powers."

"Don't start with that, Tyler. I already hear it enough from this guy."

Mr. Diaz sniffed and rubbed his nose with the back of his hand. Tyler waited for the restaurateur to speak, but he didn't say anything. He might not have been listening to them at all. The wind picked up, fanning notebook pages. The cumulus clouds had floated off to cooler climes, unleashing a heavy wash of sunlight that instantly bleached color from the parking lot. Tyler squinted.

"How'd this begin, anyway?"

Rosa Diaz fanned herself with a magazine. "How did what begin?"

"The town, I mean. Wormwood."

Rosa sat back again. "Oh, you know. Like every town in Nevada. Some trusting Indians show a white man where the gold is, then the white man gets excited and starts digging. I think Wormwood became a town in the 1850s, not too long after the gold rush out in California."

"Do they still mine gold?"

"No. That dried up a long time ago. The new deal is copper. I guess there's a big seam of it in the mountains."

Angela and Izel Diaz came out of Taco Thunder, shading their eyes against the glare. Rosa waved to her daughters. They waved back and headed toward the shelter. "You'll have to deal with these two soon enough," Rosa said to Tyler. "If they give you any trouble in class, let me know about it."

"I'm sure they'll be fine, Rosa."

"I want them to listen. I want them to educate themselves."

"It does not matter," Mr. Diaz said. "Anything they learn will be unlearned soon enough. The Meteor will see to that."

Rosa swore under her breath. She leaned far back in her chair and squeezed her eyes shut, hugging herself as she rocked. The Diaz sisters came up and stood in front of the shelter, their round faces solemn as they studied the adults. No one spoke. The sky behind the girls was so blue it seemed to buzz, as if the entire firmament hung on a frame of blue neon tubing. Tyler looked at his watch. Another five minutes and they'd head back to school.

After class, Tyler went home and sat in the backyard with a glass of iced tea and seven final essays. The sun had swung round to the west and the entire backyard, including the swinging bench, was in the shade. A grasshopper jumped from spot to spot, trying to get comfortable. Tyler picked the first essay up and set the rest beside him on the bench, placing a smooth gray stone on top of the papers to keep them from blowing away. He pushed off with his feet, setting the bench into motion, and smoothed the essay out on his leg. Handwritten and messy, it ran a surprising five pages long. The author was Bernard Tell, otherwise known as Skull. Tyler read the essay straight through, without pausing to mark it.

THE METEOR

So. A meteor fell through our atmosphere but didn't break up, even though it caught fire. It landed in the middle of town and woke everyone up. I was already up. I was practicing my bass in my bedroom with the headphones on, and even I heard the meteor hit. I thought for sure it was a bomb at first. You know, terrorists.

I went downstairs. Mom was in the kitchen. She was only wearing a skank top and underwear. I yelled at her to get some clothes on, what if that was a chemical bomb and they had to evacuate the whole town. While she was getting dressed I got one of my dad's beers from the fridge and pounded the whole thing, right there. He wasn't home. He was downtown at the bar, like every night. He works for the mining company driving a haul truck. He works six days a week and spends Sunday on the couch, watching sports. He doesn't give a crap about anything. Seriously.

I put my shoes on and went outside. Everybody's lights were on now. You could hear doors slamming and dogs barking and people were standing outside in their pajamas. I called my girlfriend on her cell phone but the network was overloaded from everybody having the same idea. My mom came out of the house and we walked downtown together toward the dirt cloud. It was hard to believe all the people walking with us. I had no idea Wormwood had so many people. Walking around town, you'd think about two dozen people lived here. It's so empty, right? But everybody and their mom came out to see what exploded.

At first it was hard to see with all the dirt and crap in the air. I pulled my shirt up over my mouth to breathe easier. Some guys from the city started digging in the crater. They uncovered this huge rock. A meteor. Or a meteorite. I didn't know the difference at first, but a meteor is what it's called when it's flying through space and meteorite is what it's called after it lands. The meteorite looked like it was part metal. I asked my dad about it later he said it was probably mostly made up of nickel iron, and that's how it survived falling through our atmosphere. Falling stars are usually meteors burning up, and the ones that burn up fastest are just made of stone, no metal.

I found my girlfriend Bratt in the crowd and we chilled for an hour, hanging around while everybody got drunk at the crater and acted like idiots. Bratt got cold, so we left before they found Mr. Diaz in the drugstore Dumpster. My mom told me about him the next day when we had choco- late chip waffles for lunch. She makes pretty good waffles.

Mr. Diaz says the world is about to be destroyed by a meteor even bigger than the one that wiped out the dinosaurs. Everybody says the meteor landing cracked his brain and turned him crazy, but I don't think so anymore. I've gone over there with my girlfriend a couple of times and talked with him. He doesn't seem that crazy. Not any crazier than my uncle, who got exposed to some of that poison gas in the Persian Gulf War and spends most of his time riding his dirt bike in the mountains and hunting coyotes and bobcats with a Berretta 92 semiautomatic handgun stuffed in his shorts. Mr. Diaz focuses on you when you talk and listens to what you have to say. So what if he likes sitting outside 24/7 in his recliner? It's a free country.

I think Mr. Diaz just wants to believe the world is about to end because that's more interesting than spending the rest of your life running a crappy restaurant in a crappy small town in the middle of nowhere. You know what I mean? Every once in a while, I wouldn't mind the world ending, either. It would be the coolest thing anyone has ever seen in the history of Earth, right? And if you saw something like that, maybe your life would actually mean something besides the fact that you showed up, had some sex, worked for a bunch of decades before you finally croaked in an old folks' home with oatmeal spilling out of your mouth. The end of the world would be like the night the meteor landed downtown, times a million.

Tyler slid Skull's essay back under the paperweight stone, on top of the others. He took a drink from his sweating glass of iced tea and decided to read the rest later. He could only take so much.

TWENTY

Arriving home from work three days after her G-men grocery store sighting, Anna found her in-law napping, kicked back in her recliner and covered with a pink and teal afghan that practically screamed fashion crime. Roscoe lay snoring at Bernie's feet, his furry right foreleg twitching as he bounded through his dreams. Anna went into the kitchen. Sunlight beamed through the kitchen windows and reflected off the oven door. The bright light made Anna's head hurt. She imagined herself turning on the gas, opening the oven door, and kneeling in front of the stove like a religious supplicant. She'd breathe the fumes deeply until her mind slowed, then darkened entirely. She could see the newspaper headline now:

EX-NEBRASKAN BEAUTY QUEEN OFFS
HERSELF IN IN-LAW'S KITCHEN

Anna smirked and got a banana strawberry yogurt out of the fridge. She ate it while standing at the counter and paging through a copy of *Flying Saucer Review* Bernie had left out. She didn't understand how anyone could believe this crap. UFOs in Cuba. UFOs in Hawaii. Why did space aliens get to travel to all the most exotic locations? How did they manage to take all that time off from work?

Anna tossed her empty yogurt cup in the trash and went up to her room. She felt like lying down.

In this nightmare, Bernie's living room was empty and the TV displayed nothing but static. The unit was covered with dust, and so was the framed picture of Leonard Nemoy sitting on top of it. Anna swiped her hand across the TV screen and stared at her fingerprints. They looked like claw marks.

The pea-green couch and matching armchairs were covered with dust, too. Anna swatted the couch cushions. Dust motes rose into the air and sifted down again. Anna went into the dining room, the kitchen. Dust coated every surface. It reminded her of pictures she'd seen of Pompeii, of the ash-people buried alive by a volcano's sudden eruption. Is that what happened here? Anna followed her own footprints in the dust, retracing her steps to the empty living room. She went into the front hall, took a deep breath, and stepped outside. She instinctively dug in her heels and dropped her hands, bracing herself for Roscoe's rambunctious greeting, but the charge didn't come. The yard was empty. No dust here, though the rocky patch of sand Bernie called a front yard was unusually thick with weeds. Gray clouds darkened the sky. A cold wind rustled the weeds as Anna stepped into the yard. None of the neighbors were outside, but that wasn't so unusual. The front gate squealed as she pulled it open and squealed again when she shut it. She walked around town.

Wormwood High School was empty. Empty hallways, empty lockers, empty auditorium. Tyler's classroom was empty, the papers piled on his desk yellowed and crumbling. The Lucky Coyote's slot machines were dark, the stools unoccupied by Anna's dependable, chain-smoking regulars. Main Street was deserted. The post office, the grocery store, and even the bar were dark, shades drawn, floors covered with dust, layers and layers of dust molded into dunes by the occasional draft of air. Even Mr. Diaz's ratty brown recliner had been abandoned beside the meteorite crater, the wooden roof of his three-sided shelter sagging inward, nearing collapse.

Anna leaned over the crater's edge. The meteorite was partially hidden under windblown sand. Eventually, it would be buried along with the rest of the town. The desert was going to swallow all of this. The desert would swallow the meteorite and then, with no one around to comprehend the long, blazing journey it had made across space, the meteorite would become just another rock in an underworld stuffed with rocks.

Anna backed away from the crater and returned across town to her in-law's house. She lay down on the pea-green couch in the living room. She watched spiders cover the ceiling in a gauze of silver and white, creating a series of patterns that grew more and more intricate as time passed, as if the spiders were constantly trying to outdo themselves and wanted her to judge their work, to tell them if it was good enough and allow them, at last, to stop and rest.

Dust filled the house. It rose to the couch, then to her side. It settled on her legs and covered her chest while her empty stomach hardened from within. Dust trickled down the back of her throat, filtering into her lungs, until it was all she could do not to cough.

Anna woke to find her husband standing by the bed, watching her. He had a bouquet of yellow daisies clasped between both hands, like a flower girl at a wedding. He stood back on his heels, as if he'd been patiently waiting for her to wake up. He held out the bouquet. She pressed the flowers against her nose and their perfume filled her mind with color. The vast emerald jungles of South America. The deep opal seas of the Atlantic. Anna drew her husband toward her and, recalling the cold ghost town of her dreams, pressed her body against his.

"Tyler, I want to do something. I want to have sex in the crater."

They folded two blankets and sat at the dining room table, drinking rum and Cokes while they waited for the sun to set and leave the town in peace. Bernie had left with the other Hairnets for their monthly trip to the Silverton Mall, and Roscoe slept under the dining room table. Time seemed to have frozen. The light outside didn't get any darker or any brighter. Tyler kept drinking, for the liquid courage as much as anything.

Anna pushed her chair back from the table. "Let's go."

"We haven't had dinner yet."

"I'm not hungry."

"That rum is going to hit you hard without any food in your stomach. I could make spaghetti."

"No. Let's just go."

Anna stood up and hugged her blanket to her chest. She stared directly ahead, as if she could see through the wall. Her beauty was undeniable, radiating from her smooth skin, her arctic blue eyes, and the firm set of her chin. She would lead the way into action, and the only sensible thing to do was follow.

Mr. Diaz sat alone and gave no sign that he noticed the couple as they joined him in his shelter. Tyler folded his hands on the blanket in his lap and scanned the street. It was a Friday night like any other Friday night in Nevada. A truck drifted down Main Street. Tyler watched it pass, wondering if its driver suspected them of anything. Tyler felt watched. The stars watched them. The moon watched them. The whole universe knew what was about to happen.

Tyler sat forward. "How you doing tonight, Mr. Diaz?"

Mr. Diaz didn't reply. Tyler glanced at his wife. She was staring ahead, zoned-out. What had she dreamt about this time? What was wrong with her?

Tyler sat back and unfolded the blanket, covering his lap. He felt around in his front pocket and took out the cigarette pack and the lighter. He lit a joint, cupping it from the wind with his hand. The first hit bloomed inside his chest, and he held it, savoring the rough particles. He blew out the smoke in Anna's direction, but she didn't respond to the provocation.

"You guys won't believe this, but I think there's an alien in town."

Another car passed on Main Street. Tyler waved, but it was too dark and he couldn't see if they waved back.

"I don't mean an illegal alien. I mean an alien from outer space. An alien from an entirely separate galaxy altogether."

Anna turned. "What?"

"He looks like your standard spaceman. He's short. About three feet tall, I guess. Gray skin. Big round head, eyes shaped like almonds. I saw him in Bernie's backyard, and then I saw him at the Fourth of July fireworks show. He was watching me, really staring. I think he either wants to abduct me or marry me. Could be both."

Tyler took another toke. Good weed. Better than average, he'd have to say.

"You saw an alien?"

Tyler nodded. "Yes, ma'am."

Anna reached over and took the joint from him. She took a toke and handed it back to him, cheeks sucked in. Smoke leaked out the side of her mouth. She exhaled, smiling for the first time that afternoon.

"You're full of crap, Ty. But I still love you."

Someone shook his shoulder. He'd fallen asleep in the folding chair and his back hurt. Anna's hair fell across his face. It smelled like oranges and wood smoke.

"Tyler, wake up. He's fallen asleep."

Tyler got out of his chair. The blanket fell off his lap and onto the parking lot. Anna picked it off the ground and shook it.

"Do you want to go first?"

"Go first?"

Anna patted his cheek. "Wake up, honey. The crater. Do you want to go first into the crater?"

"Sure."

The ground around the crater was tricky, especially in the dark. The meteor's impact had buckled the cheap asphalt pavement and made it treacherous. Tyler picked his steps carefully, glad for the moonlight. He stepped over the short rabbit fence and turned around to face his wife. She was holding both blankets against her chest and watching the sky.

"Here goes."

"Be careful."

Tyler sat down on the crater's edge and dangled his legs

over the opening. The meteorite was down there somewhere, at the bottom of the seven-foot drop, but he couldn't make it out against the pit's absolute black. He had a little flashlight on his key chain, but he didn't want to use it unless he had to. The light could give them away if anybody happened to pass by. He slid forward on the seat of his pants and dropped forward.

He landed on his feet, wavered, and caught himself on a stringy root protruding from the crater wall. He let his eyes adjust. It wasn't as dark in the crater as he thought it would be. He could make out the meteorite, anyway. It looked bigger than it did from above.

Anna's face appeared over the crater's edge. "Any problems?"

"Nope. Toss me the blankets."

Anna dropped the blankets into his arms. He unfolded one and smoothed it on the ground. He threw the second blanket on top of the first. The crater smelled like water and iron ore deposits and reminded him of a farm well.

Anna sat down on the crater's edge. Tyler reached up and took her hand. She landed much more gracefully than he had.

"Let your eyes adjust."

"Okay."

Anna took off her shoes and walked barefoot across the blanket he'd laid out. She put her hand on top of the meteorite.

"It's cold."

Tyler went over and touched the meteorite.

"What did you expect?"

"I don't know. You said it was on fire, didn't you?"

Tyler yawned. "You thought the meteorite would retain the heat from ablation? All summer? Heck, it had to fall miles and miles through the atmosphere after it caught fire. It was cold before it even landed."

"Oh." Anna put her hands behind Tyler's neck and laced her fingers together. He put his hands on her waist as she drew him toward her.

"Are you sure you want to do this, Ty?"

"Anything that helps."

"I know this isn't your usual kind of thing."

Tyler smiled and kissed his wife, slipping his hands down the small of her back and beneath the tight fabric of her jeans. She pulled him to the floor of the crater, where they undressed and drew the second blanket over them. The meteorite sat above them, silent, motionless, and close enough to touch.

The clouds came out and the stars disappeared. They watched the sky darken, still naked beneath the blanket. Anna sat up on her elbows. Even though she was beside him, Tyler could barely make out her face in the darkness. He thought she was going to say something, but she just watched the sky, propped up, her breasts resting on the swelled lip of the blanket. She could have been anyone, and, like some otherworldly creature, her expression could have signified anything.

TWENTY-ONE

Tyler got up early the next morning. He stood in the kitchen while he waited for the coffee to brew and ate a bowl of Fruit Loops. Roscoe came into the kitchen, allowed himself to be petted, and padded into the living room to fall back asleep. Tyler finished eating and set his bowl in the sink. The coffeepot clicked off. Tyler poured himself a cup and thought about his wife, who'd started tossing around four A.M. and had moved to the bedroom floor shortly after, the bed's comforter wound around her body like a cotton shell, her pillow chucked across the room. No, last night hadn't solved anything. The nightmares weren't going anywhere. Was it time to make some calls to Silverton? They'd have psychologists there, with experience and resources Tyler, as well as Wormwood, just couldn't offer.

Tyler went into the living room and got his hiking shoes on, stepping over Roscoe on his way to the front hall. He went outside and sat on the front steps, finishing his coffee as the sky changed from dark to light blue, the mountains above town gradually sharpening as the sun rose. That was a red you didn't see in Nebraska. That mineral, mountain red.

A pickup truck turned onto their street and headed for the house. Tyler finished his coffee and set it to the far edge of the steps, where it would be out of the way. He stood and watched the truck pull up. Roscoe woke and came scrabbling to the front door, pawing at the glass to be unleashed upon the sleeping world. Tyler left the dog inside the house and went through the yard, latching the front gate behind him. The truck's passenger door popped open and Tyler hauled himself up. Clyde Ringston nodded to him from the driver's seat. "Morning, Ty."

They drove through the town's empty streets and headed south on a gravel road. Clyde had a blue cooler in the truck's backseat. Tyler lifted the cooler's lid and saw that it was filled with water, beer, and generic diet cola. He dropped the lid and sank back into his seat. A half mile outside of town, Clyde turned off the gravel road and kept going. As the truck rocked on its springs Tyler took off his sunglasses and polished them with his shirttail. A stack of books on meteorites lay between them on the truck's front seat, bookmarked and well thumbed.

"We're going to find ourselves a meteorite, Ty. Today is the day."

"You think we'll have luck our first day out?"

"Why not?"

"We've got a lot of ground to cover. It might take a few weeks before we run into anything."

"Sure," Clyde said, slowing the truck to a stop, "but there's no law that says we can't get lucky. Hell, I'm due for some good luck." Clyde turned off the ignition and they listened to the engine knock twice and fall silent. Clyde reached into the backseat and brought out a baseball cap that read GOLD MINE INSURANCE and a khaki jungle safari hat. Tyler laughed.

"Those are some stylish hats."

"Arleen hated them. Which one you want?"

"I'll take the insurance cap, Dr. Livingston."

Clyde threw him the insurance cap and punched up the safari hat. He pulled it on as if he wore it every day and grinned. "This is how we roll in Wormwood, Tyler. You might as well get used to it."

They'd started early to avoid the worst of the heat, but by nine o'clock it didn't really matter. Heat was heat, and the desert in late August had plenty of it. Tyler stuck to water, Clyde to beer, and their hats absorbed wave after wave of sweat as they walked carefully through the rocky public land, none of it valuable enough to be owned by private parties. Gnarled smoke trees and prickly pear dotted the landscape. Tyler, wearing shorts, gave the vegetation a healthy amount of space as he picked his way through the spiked terrain, eyes and ears open for scorpions, rattlesnakes, and anything else that could bring a man down. Clyde moved more casually, swaying from side to side, kicking the smaller rocks out of his way as he consulted the color photographs he'd taken of the meteorite, hoping to find a match.

The sun rose higher in the sky. They circled back to the truck, crossed the area off their county map, and drove on. They made three more stops like the first, none successful, and paused for lunch. Clyde had also brought gas station ham sandwiches and a bag of potato chips. They ate at the top of a hill, looking down on a godforsaken ranch house and the sagging buildings that surrounded it. A vulture soared high above the truck, waiting for the vehicle (or something inside of it) to die. Clyde shoved a handful of chips into his mouth and chewed, his forehead creased as he watched the vulture circle.

"Hard to believe, ain't it, Ty?"

"What's hard to believe?"

"Damn meteor landing in town. Right smack-dab in the center. Out of all this land and space, it landed in Mr. Diaz's parking lot."

"Yeah," Tyler said. "What are the odds?"

"Slim to none, buddy. Slim to none. Almost makes you think there's some reasoning behind it."

"Like what?"

"Damn if I know," Clyde said, tearing another hunk from his sandwich. "I'm just saying it's plenty strange. Nothing ever happens in Wormwood. I mean nothing. Hell, even the government would forget about us if it didn't want our taxes so bad."

A trail of dust rose to the southeast as three vehicles barreled down the gravel road that led up to the distant ranch house. Clyde opened the truck's glove compartment and pulled out a pair of binoculars. He studied the vehicles as they drew closer. "Looks like two squad cars from the sheriff's department and one black, mystery SUV. They're not wasting any time getting where they're going."

The vehicles closed in on the ranch. Two men came out of the house and stared down the road, toward the plumes of dust. They went back into the house. Clyde handed Tyler the binoculars and started the truck.

"Let's go get a better look, shall we?"

"Ah—"

"C'mon, Ty. You don't want to miss the action. They're about to bust somebody for something."

"That's okay. I'm cool with missing it."

The truck bounced as Clyde put it in gear and started rolling down the hillside, pointing the truck's hood toward the ranch house as if getting there simply required nothing more than driving in a straight line. Tyler checked his seatbelt and pushed his feet against the floor. "If Anna knew I was doing this, she'd kill me."

Clyde waved the comment off and put the truck into second gear. The tires churned on the loose soil but had enough traction to keep them moving. Ahead, the police caravan had already pulled into the ranch house's front yard. Men jumped out of the vehicles, carrying guns.

Clyde smiled and pushed the truck's accelerator to the floor. He looked happier than Tyler had ever seen him.

They made it down the hillside, avoiding the major rocks and depressions, and skidded to a stop at the end of the ranch's long gravel driveway. The sun was high and showed the entire scene in spotlight brilliance as Tyler studied the ranch through the binoculars, adjusting the lenses to increase their clarity. Beside the two-story farmhouse there was an old red barn, a small shed that might have held a water pump, and an empty, weed-chocked corral.

"What's the headcount, Ty?"

"There's five Feds with automatic rifles and S.W.A.T. gear, or whatever you call it. Two agents just went around back of the barn and the other three are spread out around the front."

"What about the cops?"

"I can see Merritt and two deputies. They're back behind the squad cars. They've got rifles trained on the house. I guess they're covering the Feds."

"Sounds like a party."

Tyler lowered the binoculars. Clyde had gotten out of the truck and was standing beside it, loading shells into a shotgun. The combination of the safari hat and the firearm made Tyler nervous.

"Where did you get that, Clyde?"

"I keep it the truck. Sometimes you run into bobcats out here."

"You're an insurance salesman."

"That doesn't mean I don't know how to shoot a gun or lend a hand."

"You're going to get yourself shot."

Clyde pumped the shotgun, loading the first shell. He winked at Tyler and shut the driver's-side door. "No offense, Ty, but you sound like my ex-wife."

"Clyde—"

"You don't have to come with me. Stay with the truck. Things get messy, feel free to scoot back to town."

Clyde pulled down the brim of his hat and walked across the front of the truck. He dropped into the ditch and strode up the other side, toward the ranch. Tyler had a hard time believing any of this was happening. Ten minutes ago they'd been hot, bored, and eating gas station ham sandwiches, two amateur geologists passing the time on a Saturday in central Nevada.

Clyde turned and waved to the truck. Tyler stepped out.

"What?"

"Come over here a sec. I think I found something."

Tyler took off his cheap advertising cap and wiped his forehead with the back of his hand. "Are you serious, Clyde?"

"Yeah. Come here already."

Tyler crossed the ditch and ran up the other side. He jogged in a crouch, keeping his eyes on the ranch. Nobody had made a move yet. The Feds had their guns trained on the barn and were still approaching slowly. The cops peered through their rifle scopes, watching the house and the yard. Tyler found Clyde on his knees, his shotgun propped up against a bush. He had his hands in the sandy soil and was digging out a piece of black rock. He noticed Tyler crouched beside him and laughed. "This is it, man. It's a fragment."

Tyler kneeled beside the insurance salesman and helped him dig. The rock's exposed end was sharp and the rest of it was stubbornly stuck into the ground. Tyler laced his hands together and pulled the rock toward him, rocking it back and forth as Clyde continued digging out handfuls of sand. Finally it gave, sliding out of the ground like a pulled tooth, and Tyler fell backward with the rock on his chest. It felt cool through the fabric of his shirt, heavier than your average paperweight. Tyler lifted it above his body and studied it in the sunlight. About a foot in length, one end of the rock was blunt and thick, like the bottom of a screwdriver, and the other end was needle sharp. It had four sides and three of the sides were rough, almost jagged. One side was totally smooth, like something that had been worn down by the intense heat of ablation. Tyler laughed. He didn't need to see pictures of the meteorite downtown. This was it. They'd found a fragment.

"You're right, Clyde. Here's your good luck."

Tyler handed the rock over to Clyde. He sat up and shaded his eyes. On the ranch, the Feds were finally moving in, running toward the barn at a sprint. Clyde held the fragment in front of his chest and was examining its sharp tip as the barn exploded behind him, going up in a spectacular ball of fire and splintered wood. The sound and the heat from the explosion crossed the ranch's front yard and slammed into them like a wave, throwing Clyde forward. As he fell, the meteorite fragment wedged itself between the insurance salesman and the earth, impaling his heart. Tyler's head snapped back as the concussion washed over them, his sunglasses flying off his face. He closed his eyes as a second explosion followed the first, and then another. Tyler pictured each ball of fire as it went up, harsh and brilliant, and the federal agents lying prone in the ranch yard, their armor fused into their skin. The barn must have housed a meth lab, Tyler decided. Nothing else would have gone up quite that way.

Thus, a union of two similar asteroids results in a family of asteroids all traveling in roughly the same orbit. This idea of asteroid families became a recognized fact in 1918 when Kiyotsugu Hirayama in Japan showed that three groups of known asteroids have similar orbital characteristics. He referred to them as families because he correctly believed that they were originally a single body that had suffered catastrophic disruption in the past. A recently disrupted family tends to orbit in a tight cluster, but as the family ages, the cluster members slowly separate from each other.

—O. Richard Norton, *Rocks From Space*

BOOK III

METEORITE DAYS

Clyde Ringston's funeral was held the following Tuesday afternoon at the Wormwood Methodist Church. The service was well attended, the chapel overflowing with fragrant funeral sprays. Clyde had sold a lot of insurance to a lot of people. The mourners talked about how friendly he'd been, how reliable. Clyde had a nice smile. Clyde looked you in the eye and shook your hand firmly. The building's air conditioner had failed that morning and the temperature inside the church was sweltering, even with the windows open and the ceiling fans turning. The crowd shifted in the hard oak pews, fanning themselves with a program celebrating Clyde's life as the old wood cracked and settled beneath them. Anna and Tyler Mayfield sat in the second row with their aunt, Bernie Turner. All three wore glazed expressions, as if stunned by the suffocating heat and unsure of exactly what was happening.

The cherry wood coffin was closed. Clyde's ex-wife sat in the front row with her boyfriend. Anna studied Arleen's fluffy red hair as Arleen wept and leaned against her new boy-friend's shoulder. How did she get so much body? Would it be rude to ask what shampoo and conditioner she used? One of Clyde's coworkers at the insurance agency stood up and began a stiff eulogy that could have been about anyone. Anna noticed Merritt Jackson looking down the row at them and nodded hello. The sheriff nodded back, unsmiling. The law-man had turned into a local legend overnight. The story went that after the meth lab's explosion, which had been triggered by the drug dealers in a last-ditch effort to destroy the evidence against them, the sheriff had walked up to the ranch house alone and entered the premises. While the police deputies dragged the injured DEA agents away from the roaring chemical fire (two dead, three still in critical condition), they heard a series of shots coming from inside the house. A moment later Merritt Jackson walked back outside, grim and uninjured. Three armed men lay dead inside, shot cleanly in the forehead.

Anna shivered and turned her attention back to the service. The coworker was still going on about a sense of community and serving the public. His brown linen suit had seen better days. Anna could see specks of lint on his shoulders, even from fifteen feet away. She wondered if the coworker had a wife and if he did why she hadn't seen the lint and how Clyde Ringston had died the instant the meteorite fragment pierced his heart. Snap. Just like that. Anna put her hand over her chest, trying to imagine what dying like that would feel like. The rock would be cold and smooth, almost slippery, and about as heavy as a two-month-old. That wave of hot air would pick you off your feet and send you flying, right into the rock's sharp end, and maybe you'd have a second to realize that you were about to die before you felt the rock rip through the fabric of your shirt and punch into your chest, cracking your ribs apart as it shoved on through to your soft, frightened heart.

The pew creaked as Tyler bent over and stared into the floor. Anna put her hand on the middle of his back and massaged it in circles, kneading his muscles with the palm of her hand. Poor guy. First his bother disappearing when he was only a kid and now his friend, dying right beside him. Tyler hadn't gotten up again after the explosion. He'd just crawled over to Clyde, checked his pulse, and lay back staring up at the sky while the barn burned and shots were fired. Merritt had told Anna at the hospital that they wouldn't have noticed Clyde and Tyler lying there if it hadn't been for the vultures circling over them, sniffing out some dinner. For three days now Tyler had barely spoken to anyone. He just sat in the backyard on the bench swing, drinking and smoking weed. Anna wanted him to call his mother in Omaha and tell her about what had happened, but he wouldn't. He said he didn't want to worry her.

The coworker finished his eulogy and sat down. The pastor continued the service, asked them to open their hymnals, and they sang "On Eagle's Wings" while the flowers wilted and sweat beaded on the congregation's foreheads and trickled down their necks. Anna wondered how the locals could stand this heat, year after year, summer after summer. They had warm summers in Nebraska, with their share of humidity, heat, and windless, mosquitoed days where even the cornstalks didn't move, but the sun here was ridiculous, like looking into the angry eye of God himself. How could you grow up with that sun beating down on you as soon as you left the house? What would that do to your mind, to your soul?

The hymn ended, the pastor gave a benediction, and the congregation started to file out, Clyde's ex-wife leading the way. Anna and Bernie started for the center aisle along with everyone else and Anna was halfway to the exit before she realized her husband wasn't following them. Tyler was still sitting in their pew, staring at the floor. His face was red from the explosion. When she'd first seen him lying in the Silverton hospital, he'd looked as if he'd fallen asleep in a tanning bed. She'd fallen on him like a woman in a hospital soap opera, weeping and hugging him until he woke up, grimacing from her weight, and she could not believe herself, acting like that. Here she was, all composure lost, the veil of dignity she'd accumulated like armor from years in the pageant circuit ripped apart by this man, this boy-man stupid enough to get caught up in the middle of a meth lab bust when he should have been miles away, minding his own business. The whole thing was ridiculous. She was an adult. Depending on someone else only made you weaker, only gave the world a chink in your armor. She wasn't going to be like her mother, tied to a scrabbling dusty farmer who was himself tied to a dusty scrabbling farm in the middle of an overfertilized plain, flat as fuck, the most exciting moment in their shared days that moment when her father opened the back door at the end of day, sat down on his grandfather's chair, and removed his boots in the mud room before heading in to his office to check the weather forecast and the ag report. No. Anna Lynette Mayfield was meant to do more than that. She was meant to do something special, and winning the Miss Nebraska pageant had only been the start. She wasn't going to be like that damn meteor, streaking through the night sky for a couple of beautiful, fiery seconds before crashing to the earth and going cold forever. She'd just started rising through the atmosphere. She was only twenty-seven, and this lightly burned man in a hospital bed would not be allowed to drag her back down.

Tyler heard her coming back down the aisle and sat up. He smiled and got to his feet, the wooden pew creaking from the sudden release of weight. Anna stood at the end of the row, adjusting the purse on her shoulder. This had been only her third funeral. The first one had been for her grandfather, whom she could no longer remember clearly, and the second had been for a girl she'd barely known in high school, who'd been killed by a drunk driver. When they went to the bar later, Clyde wouldn't be there, sitting on his favorite stool, drinking gin and beer. This was the loss that made her husband's eyes red and bleary as he walked toward her, trying to smile like he had to be brave just for her, the poor sensitive little wifey. Anna pivoted and looked down the center aisle, to the rear of the stifling church and the mourners emptying out into the sunny street, the middle-aged men lending elbows to their tottering elderly mothers as they slowly descended the church steps. She could hardly stand any of it.

TWENTY-THREE

The Wormwood Visitation Society met the day after the funeral. Ray Boones, Lila Fanon, Bernie Turner, and Tyler Mayfield sat in Felix Hill's living room, drinking coffee and eating sugar cookies while they waited for Felix to start the show. They sat in a ring of mismatched armchairs, facing one another, but any attempt at conversation stalled as soon as it began, and the house was quiet except for Felix's footsteps creaking overhead as he prepared for the meeting. Tyler wondered several times why he had come, what he expected to get out of this meeting. He gazed out the window, although it was past eight o'clock and already dark outside. He could have been at home right now, drinking himself into oblivion in the back garden.

The footsteps moved across the ceiling, turned, and descended the stairway on the other side of the house. Bernie cleared her throat and glanced at Tyler, smiling when he met her glance. More creaking steps and Felix Hill appeared beneath the living room doorway, dressed in an immaculately pressed navy blue suit, pink face buffed to a shine. He took in the room with glittering eyes and stepped inside the armchair circle. "Thank you for coming, everyone. I know you must have questions for me."

The others murmured. Tyler was confused. He didn't know he was supposed to have questions.

"A local man has died. Tragically, before his time, and the manner of his death has stained a piece of the Wormwood meteorite with blood. What can this mean, you may have asked yourself. Could we have been mistaken about the meteorite's meaning all along? Perhaps the meteorite has nothing to do with the Visitors at all. Its landing in Wormwood may simply be a coincidence, a strange quirk of fate that Felix, silly old Felix, may have misread, seeing only what he wanted to see after years spent waiting."

Felix laced his hands together and dropped them to his waist. His smile disappeared. He looked around the room, holding each person's gaze for several seconds before sliding to the next person. Tyler felt the fine hairs on his forearms lift from his skin. "You could be right," Felix said, nodding. "I could be wrong. But, I ask you, if a meteorite landing in the center of town is not sufficient evidence of contact, what are you waiting for? A postcard from Alpha Centauri? A notarized letter from the sun?"

Ray Boones raised his hand. "So what does the blood mean? Are we talking human sacrifice here?"

"Ray, I don't fully comprehend your meaning—"

"Do the Visitors want us to stab a few more people to show them we're serious?"

Felix's mouth slipped open. "Good lord, Ray. That's exactly the opposite of what the Visitors want from us. They're coming to usher in an age of peace and prosperity."

"So we don't have to sacrifice more people?"

"No," Felix said, his voice rising. "No sacrifices."

Lila drummed her nails against her coffee cup. "Felix, what do you think Clyde's death meant, then? Was he unclean?"

"No, Lila. It does not mean any such thing. I don't know where you'd get such an idea."

"Clyde was a good guy," Tyler said, looking back out the window. "He liked to talk and have a few drinks."

The conversation drifted, circling around Clyde's personality and how his death would affect Meteorite Days, which started on Friday. Tyler watched rain dot the windows and dribble down, curving patterns across the glass. He could see Clyde's face, eyes wide with surprise at his own death.

"You know," Tyler said, standing up and looking around the room, "even if the Visitors arrive tomorrow, life will still go on pretty much as it has before. The Visitors aren't going to wave a magic space wand and make everything perfect. We'll still have to go grocery shopping. We'll still have to do the laundry and go to work and watch our friends and family die around us."

Felix Hill loosened the knot on his tie and nodded. "Of course, Tyler. I never meant to imply they'd possess magic wands."

"So why should I care if they show up or not?"

"It's a question of history, Tyler. Their very appearance would be of such historical import that it would affect humanity for the rest of its existence. Humanity would know, categorically, that it was no longer alone in the universe."

Tyler tossed back the rest of his coffee and set his cup on the coffee table. "Felix, whether there's other life in the universe or not, we're all still alone. Right now, everyone in this room is alone in his skin. Just look at Clyde. I was right beside him when he died, but I might as well have been on another planet for all the comfort I could offer him. How would the Visitors change that?"

"Honestly, I don't know," Felix said, looking from Tyler to rest of the room. "By definition, their ways are alien to us. Yet who can say they won't possess a collective consciousness, a highly evolved group mind capable of reaching out to us in our infinite loneliness? They may have advanced well beyond religion, which we've used for so many generations to get along, to function as a spiritual stopgap that convinces us to continue living, that life is worthwhile, and perhaps they will explain to us how we may advance ourselves, until either we no longer feel alone or it truly ceases to bother us."

Tyler sat down again in his armchair. His aunt was staring at him as if she'd never seen him before. "You think humanity will listen to a message like that? It doesn't seem like the world's ready for that sort of fundamental change. That sounds hard. That sounds like a lot of homework. The world would probably prefer to fire some missiles, watch the explosion on the evening news, and keep doing its own thing."

Felix tugged at his coat sleeves and smiled. "Of course it will be a challenge, Tyler. But that's where the Wormwood Visitation Society comes in. We'll help facilitate that change. When the moment finally arrives, we'll act as midwives to the next brave new world."

Tyler drove around Wormwood after the society meeting with no particular direction in mind. Eventually he found himself pulled toward the town hall, a modest, one-story adobe building on the north end of Main Street. Town hall housed the city council, the mayor's office, and the sheriff's department. Tyler parked in the empty lot next to the building and walked up the front sidewalk. He'd been here just two nights before, giving eyewitness evidence regarding the meth lab bust and Clyde Ringston's death. Already that interview seemed like a long time ago, something that had happened to a younger version of Tyler Mayfield.

He entered the building and paused to adjust to the chilled air and bright, fluorescent lights. The wall to his right was covered with wooden and brass plaques, honors given to members of the police force and the general community. Desert landscape paintings, a stuffed owl, and a six-foot-tall laminated map of Nevada decorated the wall to his left. Tyler found Wormwood on the map and circled it with his finger. You Are Here. He continued down the corridor, the rubber soles of his shoes squeaking on the waxed marble floor. The sheriff's department was at the end of the hall, to the left, and its door was open. Tyler knocked and stepped inside.

"Hello?"

The room contained a small office, with four desks and another doorway that led to the storage rooms and the holding cells. A young man around Tyler's age was sitting behind a desk at the back of the room, wearing a headset. He reclined in his chair, hands laced behind his head as he watched something on his computer monitor. Joey, Tyler remembered. The nightshift dispatcher. Grew up surfing in California.

"Is Merritt here?"

"No, sir. He went home about an hour ago. You want me to leave a message for him?"

Tyler looked around the office. "No, that's okay. Mind if I use your bathroom?"

"Go ahead," Joey said, waving at the air. "Just down the hall and to your right."

Tyler passed through the room as Joey went back to his porn or whatever he was watching on his computer. The hallway was narrow but well lit, with more fluorescent lights. Tyler passed a supply closet and two holding cells on his way to the bathroom, wondering why he wasn't at home already, urinating in his own bathroom. He noticed a door at the end of the hall that was slightly ajar. It had a sign on it that read EVIDENCE LOCKER and while he was in the bathroom he thought about it, this open door. When he left the bathroom the hallway was still empty, and the door was still ajar, so Tyler decided to check it out.

He didn't know what to expect, maybe gallon Ziplocs full of weed, confiscated from desert drug lords, but the evidence locker was just a small room lined with wire shelves. Most of the shelves were empty, though one shelf was filled with carefully labeled plastic bags holding empty bullet casings, something charred, and one sliver of rock. Tyler glanced over his shoulder at the empty hallway and stepped inside the room. He lifted the plastic bag with the rock off the shelf and held it against the light, turning the rock to different angles. The fragment was so dark it seemed to deflect light, even in this small, artificially illuminated room. Tyler had expected it to be coated with a lacquer of rich, coppery red, but the fragment appeared untouched by Clyde's bloody death.

Tyler wrapped the plastic bag tightly around the meteorite and shoved its pointed end into his front pocket and covered the rest of it with his T-shirt. He turned off the evidence locker's overhead light and started back down the hallway. He'd just passed the bathroom door when Joey appeared, smiling.

"Hey, man. I was about to send out a search party for you."

"Sorry. We had Mexican tonight."

"So you really pounded it, huh?"

"I wouldn't go in there for a while if I were you."

Joey laughed and walked with him back to the front office. Tyler stuck his hands in his front pocket, trying to conceal the bulge on his right hip. The meteorite's weight seemed to increase with each step, threatening to burst the fabric of his cargo shorts and fall clattering to the floor. Joey slapped Tyler on the back and told him to have a good night. Tyler kept walking, wondering at the absurdity of it all, at the absurdity of stealing something from the police evidence locker knowing full well they'd have no suspects for the theft other than him, that eventually they'd come knocking on his door wanting an answer. And what would he say to them when they came with their search warrants and guns drawn? That it was all a whim? A crazy stupid whim? That he'd seen a drinking buddy die in front of him as the sky exploded, illegal chemicals detonating, a blistering heat wave onrushing, and then the sound of distant, muffled gunfire as more men died inside an aging farmhouse while Tyler's other drinking buddy walked among them, gun blazing? That he'd stolen government property because of a blue sky and the vultures circling overhead, waiting to pry into his ropy intestines, to dig in with their hooked beaks like mad carnivore surgeons?

Tyler strode out of the police department and back down the gleaming hall, past the maps and citations of valor, and into the dry evening. The Nevada sky twinkled above him— so many stars—and he dropped into the front seat of his car. Tyler tossed the fragment of meteorite on the passenger seat and drove home slowly, stopping for an old tabby cat as it sprinted across the street, orange fur sprung, its green eyes feral with the night.

TWENTY-FOUR

On the Friday before Labor Day weekend, Anna and Tyler took Roscoe downtown to watch the carnies set up shop for Meteorite Days. Four blocks of Main Street had been closed for the town festival. The southernmost block contained a Tilt-a-Whirl, an octopus, an inflatable Velcro wall, and, of course, a Ferris wheel. Anna also noticed a small stable across the street, where a skinny pony stood beneath a pavillion, watching the other carnival rides with dull eyes. The second city block was crammed with food trailers painted bright pinks and yellows, their signs promising cotton candy, fried minidoughnuts, hamburgers, hot dogs, syrup-flavored ice, and steak kebabs. The food trailers were placed unevenly along the street, instead of in one long row, making it necessary for carnivalgoers to weave through the maze to pass on through. The second block also had a line of six white-roofed, aquamarine portapotties, their shiny plastic bodies already baking in the sun.

The beer garden occupied the next two blocks of Main Street, its boundaries clearly delineated by an orange plastic fence to keep the underaged out. The beer garden's setup men dragged picnic tables into haphazard clumps. On the east side, a large bartender's tent had been raised. Beyond the picnic tables and tent was an open stretch of pavement with a stage for the band. The perimeter fence ran behind the stage, enclosing the beer garden in a looping arc. Beyond the stage you could see Mr. Diaz's wooden shelter, rising from the parking lot of Taco Thunder with all the majesty of an outhouse.

"Wow," Anna said, glancing at her husband through her sunglasses. "This is some setup. I bet they would have stuffed a roller coaster in here somewhere if they could have figured out how do it on a thousand-dollar budget."

They walked around the fairgrounds, keeping to the sidewalk. Anna decided the carnival didn't seem as out of place on Main Street as she'd expected. Back in Lincoln, a setup like this would have seemed artificial, as sturdy as a snowflake, but here in Nevada it seemed downright sensible. The gold, silver, and copper deposits never lasted long, much less forever. Why not build collapsible buildings? Why not travel light, and go wherever the good times are?

Roscoe strained against his leash, nearly yanking Tyler off his feet. They'd passed the beer garden and Roscoe could smell Taco Thunder across the street. "Easy, man. Easy. We'll go say hi." Mrs. Diaz was sitting beside her husband in his shelter, fanning herself with a tabloid. Mr. Diaz, stunningly showered, shaven, and attired in a white suit, sat with his hands folded across his lap. If it wasn't for the meteorite crater they might have been your average, everyday married couple enjoying the nice weather.

Anna squatted beside Mrs. Diaz. "Your old man's looking good today, Rosa."

"It was his idea. A whole summer of not showering, and he shows up this morning wanting to be Mr. Clean."

"He even shaved."

"He thinks the end comes today. But why, I wonder, is today different from any other? Because my husband decided to bathe like a normal person? Because we're having our town festival? Nothing Charles says or does makes sense anymore. My husband might as well have died when that stupid meteor landed. Who is this freeloading bum sitting in our parking lot? You tell me."

Mr. Diaz licked his cracked lips. His face was thinner than ever, burnt from a summer of wind and sun. Anna set her hand on Mrs. Diaz's forearm.

"You're a saint, Rosa. You'll be going to heaven first class."

"It is not where I'm going that I'm worried about," Rosa said, turning to stare at her husband. "It is where my daughters are going. College will not be cheap, and keeping a lunatic fed is not cheap, either."

"He'll come around," Tyler said. "He just needs some time."

"I used to think so. But now, I don't know."

Rosa sighed. Anna stuck her hands in her rear pockets and leaned back, stretching out her vertebrae.

"We better keep moving, Rosa. See you later."

"See you," Rosa said. "Enjoy the carnival tonight."

They stopped on the way back to Bernie's beneath the shade of a tree to let Roscoe sniff a fire hydrant and leave a message of his own. Anna put a hand on Tyler's shoulder and squeezed. "Ty, let's just go back to Nebraska. In a few months, this summer will just be a crazy story we can tell at parties."

"I signed a contract, Anna. I'm teaching English this fall."

"You can break the contract. They'll forget about it and you'll get another teaching job back home."

Tyler pulled Roscoe away from the hydrant and they continued walking. "We ran away to come out here, and three months later you want to run back. That's a crappy way to live, don't you think?"

Roscoe pulled hard left, dragging Tyler off the sidewalk and into the street. Tyler walked after the dog in the gutter, his sandals thwaping against the concrete. He kept looking up at the sky as he walked, even though it was empty.

"What are you looking for, Ty?"

"Nothing."

"You're looking for the Meteor, aren't you? You think Mr. Diaz is right."

"No, I don't."

"Well, you're looking for something."

They came to the house and stopped outside the gate. Roscoe knew he was home and sat down patiently, ready to go inside. Tyler handed the dog's leash to Anna and stepped back.

"I think I'm going to keep walking. I need to think."

Anna unlatched the gate and unhooked Roscoe's leash. The dog bounded into his front yard. He lifted his leg and peed on a cactus in a clay pot. "You're going to give yourself heatstroke, Ty. Come in and get a bottle of water before you go. And some sunscreen."

"No thanks. I'm good."

Anna went into the yard and closed the gate. She watched her husband dwindle into a small figure as he headed west. She had no idea what his deal was. He didn't usually put up such a strong fight. Tyler Mayfield was a natural born pushover. As long as she'd known him, friends had been roping him into helping them move, watching their obnoxious pets, and going on uncomfortable double dates. Now he was putting his foot down, drinking too much, and going on long, strange walks by himself. This town was changing him.

Anna went upstairs to take a nap before the carnival started. The room was warm, even with the central air-conditioning, and she stripped down to her underwear before lying down on the bed. She thought about reading a maga-zine, but the stack was beyond her reach, on top of the dresser.

The bedsprings shifted beneath her as she tried to get comfortable, punching up her pillow and turning to her side. She was tired. She'd dreamt of an acid monsoon the night before, blowing in from the northern seaboard and churning into Nebraska, where it held for days, melting anyone foolish enough to go outside, gradually wearing away buildings, eroding their roofs and walls until the structures gave way totally, exposing their huddled occupants to torrents of skin-dissolving precipitation.

Anna shifted again. Something hard was pressing up through the mattress, poking her in the hip. She got out of bed and lifted up the mattress.

"What the hell?"

Someone had placed a rock in a plastic bag on the box spring. Anna picked up the bag and examined its tag. Her lower lip curled.

"Damn it, Tyler."

She hefted the meteorite fragment in one hand. It wasn't as big as she'd imagined it. The way Clyde's death had been described to her, she'd imagined the fragment as a three-foot rock spear. This was more like a chunk of rock you might find on the side of the road, not that different from the rocks around it.

Anna sat on the edge of the bed. You could go to jail for stealing police evidence, couldn't you? Anna opened the plastic bag and took the rock out. Why would Tyler want to risk jail time for this? Anna lifted the rock to her face and placed it against her cheek. Nice and cool, like the bigger meteorite downtown, with a metallic smell. She tossed the evidence bag on the floor and lay back with the meteorite at her side. She set it on her chest, between her breasts. Her heart beat against the rock's comforting weight. She closed her eyes and followed the pulse.

TWENTY-FIVE

The prospect of returning to Nebraska loomed before Tyler like a pillow-lined coffin. He walked to the western edge of town and kept going. Two kestrels took flight in front of him, crying *killy-killy* as they chased each other across the sky. The desert terrain was dotted with sagebrush, cacti, and the occasional Joshua tree. It had rained hard the day before and the precipitation had triggered an unusual late August bloom. The prickly pear colonies were covered with flowers, both pink and bronze, and the barrel cacti were crowned in buttercup yellow. Even the wormwood was covered with minute, tan flowers. Tyler leaned over and examined the shrub more closely, wondering why anyone would have wanted to name a town after such a pale, scraggly plant. Its flowers were knotted in ugly little clusters, and its leaves were covered with fine, thirsting hairs. It looked about as desperate as a plant could get.

The mountain range was a rough mile from town. To the

south, a gravel access road ran from town to the mountains, and Tyler decided to cut across the countryside and make for the road. Sunlight poured onto his skin. He should have worn a hat. He pictured Anna, shaking her head when he returned to the house sunburned. He connected with the gravel access road and continued west. He took deep, steady breaths. The road began to curve upward. Nothing moved but him.

Tyler walked up the mountain road, sweating through his shorts and T-shirt. He could no longer recall why this hike had seemed like a good idea. What could wandering into the mountains like an unprepared idiot possibly solve? Anna was right. You couldn't deny that the stars were aligned against them as well as this entire, ill-considered venture. They could return to Nebraska. A week from now they could be imposing on friends in Lincoln, hunting for a cheap apartment, and up-dating their résumés. Soon Wormwood would be nothing but a strange story to tell at parties, after the early birds left for home and the hardcore partiers settled in for serious drinking.

Of course, Tyler's older brother would not have given up so easy. Not even with the nightly apocalyptic nightmares. Not even with a friend dying right in front of him. Cody was fearless. Once, at summer camp, Cody had grabbed a copper-head snake right off the ground and sung "Sweet Caroline" into its snapping mouth, just to make everybody laugh.

The access road flattened out and went on through a

narrow valley. Tyler turned around. Wormwood looked insignificant from here. A scrubby cluster of aluminum-sided buildings and concrete. A gray strip of highway to the east, and beyond the highway just more sagebrush, as far as a person could see. In the far distance, lining the horizon like a low-hanging front of purple clouds, was the next mountain range over. You could walk from these mountains to those mountains without encountering anything except Wormwood, and that you could pass through in ten minutes.

Tyler turned around and continued down the road. He felt exposed as he walked through the valley. The hills on both sides curved like camel humps, bare except for the occasional scraggily patch of vegetation. The idea that anyone would bother to sit up there among the rocks, spying on him in this heat, was absurd. Still, he felt watched.

The road turned sharply to the left, diving into another valley. A faded metal sign had been posted on the side of the road.

FRANKLIN MINING COMPANY
Mining since 1864

Tyler patted the sign as he passed. Roughly two hundred yards beyond, the ground dropped away into an enormous open pit. The pit's walls had been carved in rough, rectangular layers, the rock burgundy red. A dump truck and an excavator sat motionless in the southwest corner, like old toys discarded in a playground sandbox. Otherwise, the pit was devoid of machines, workers, or movement. A chain-link fence had been drawn across the mouth of the gravel access road that wound down to the pit floor. Apparently, the entire Franklin Mining Company had gotten an early start on Labor Day weekend.

Tyler left the access road and picked his way across the hill. He found a flat chunk of rock beside an overgrown juniper bush and sat down. The sun was starting to drop, but that just made it feel hotter. No shade anywhere. Tyler took out his cigarette hard pack and pulled out a joint. Places like this shouldn't exist, he decided. The ground had been raped. The land was crying out, an open wound with no bandage in sight. He smoked the joint. He felt superior and alone. He wanted to roll down the side of the pit and see how fast he could go. He wanted to pull precious raw materials out of the ground with his bare hands and bring them home with him. He'd throw the rocks on the table and say, "Here. Here is a good reason to stay."

The sun dropped lower. A few clouds drifted in from the north and covered the sun the best they could. Tyler smoked a second joint to celebrate the cloud cover. His blood was bubbling beneath his skin, as if his bones had been replaced by an elaborate Jacuzzi system. He must have been sunburned and dehydrated, but he felt pretty good. He was communing with nature.

Tyler was considering heading back to town when the pit began to shift. The bottom of the pit was deep in shadows now, and at first he thought it was the wind swirling the soil around, but then the ground began moving in a very apparent way. Something was coming up from beneath the ground, pushing all the wine-red soil and rock to the side. Tyler stood up and leaned forward. The rising object was saucer-shaped and metallic and made absolutely no sound as it rose.

"Yes," Tyler said. "This is more like it."

The ship, which had a matte gray hull, drew in the hot air around it and blew out cold air, so much cold air that Tyler felt the temperature drop a good forty degrees, as if he'd stepped out of the summer afternoon and into a meat locker. The ship stopped rising when it reached Tyler's eye level. Below it, the ground was ruptured, a significant space gouged out of the pit floor. Tyler stepped forward, tripped on a rock, and almost fell down the hillside. He raised his hand.

"Hello?"

A dark circle appeared on the ship's deck. Tyler nodded.

"Yes. Yes."

A short, gray figure rose through a hatch and watched Tyler with dark eyes. The spaceman's short arms hung limp at his sides, and his hands were relaxed and empty. Tyler counted three long fingers on each hand. He couldn't see if he (she, it?) had fingernails or not. Tyler wondered if he could jump onto the ship if he backed up and took a running start. He'd like to feel that ship beneath his feet, its silent motor buzzing through the soles of his shoes. "Hello," Tyler said, waving. "Good to see you again."

The ship bobbed slightly in the air. So it wasn't totally stable after all. The laws of physics applied to even the most advanced civilizations.

"Where have you been the last two months?"

The figure didn't move.

"You haven't been living underground this whole time, have you?"

The ship bobbed again. The breeze was getting stronger, but it was hard to imagine wind affecting something this big. This was a ship built to travel across the dark reaches of outer space, with a hull built to withstand asteroid fields and solar flares and total vacuums. This ship was the safest thing around.

"Are you here to abduct me?"

The alien cocked its head.

"I guess not."

Tyler's knees loosened under him. He sat back down and touched his cheek. It was warm from sunburn. What a long summer it had been here in Nevada. A summer to end all summers.

The alien remained on the deck of his ship, tranquilly watching Tyler and in no particular hurry. Maybe it communicated by using silence, and only silence. The alien might not even have vocal cords. Ray Boones had asked once if the Visitors communicated telepathically, like he'd seen on TV, and Felix Hill had told the society that the Visitors were beyond even that. All they needed to do was look each other in the eye and they knew instantly what the other being was thinking and feeling. They were that close. They didn't have brothers, or sisters, or any type of family unit. They didn't need to break themselves up into little segments like that. The Visitors understood that it was the vehicle as a whole that mattered, a united race propelling itself across space and time toward a destiny so bright and happy the human mind staggered trying to comprehend it.

Tyler picked up a rock and hurled it at the bottom half of the ship. The rock clanged off the hull and dropped into the copper pit, falling a good five hundred feet. The alien lifted its head and gazed at the sky.

"You're not here to destroy earth, are you?"

The alien continued watching the sky. Tyler waved.

"Hello? Are you listening?"

The alien dropped his gaze and stared at Tyler with those dark, liquid eyes. Tyler shivered. The sky had turned pink and gold, and the sun was definitely starting to set. Back in town, the beer garden would have opened by now. The carnival rides would be lit up. Anna would be drinking Lite beer and laughing. People would be everywhere, stuffing their faces and making noise.

"I have to go back now," Tyler said. "Have a good night."

The alien still didn't speak. Tyler turned his back on the

hovering ship and the ring of cold air that surrounded it. He watched his feet as he walked back to the gravel access road, trying to ignore the feeling of the alien's eyes on his back. His mouth was dry and his legs unsteady beneath him; it was going to be a long walk home.

He'd done all this to himself, of course.

This had been his bright idea.

Tyler was halfway down the mountain when the spaceship appeared above his head and bobbed three times in the air, like a Frisbee flying against the wind. Tyler lifted his head and shaded his eyes. The ship bobbed once more and sped on, heading east in a gray blur. Tyler kept walking. He reached the edge of Wormwood at dusk. A woman stood in her backyard, hanging white sheets on a drooping clothesline. She noticed him and waved. Tyler returned the wave and watched the woman gather her empty clothes basket and go inside her house. His feet ached as he stepped onto a sidewalk. He couldn't remember pavement ever feeling so hard.

TWENTY-SIX

By dusk, the beer garden was packed. People crammed in front of the band stage, dancing to the amplified, four-piece country act. They stood in line at the beer tent, shouting above the music and tugging at their paper bracelets. They thronged the picnic tables, smoking and drinking and eating hamburgers. Anna sat at a table with Bernie and three of Bernie's friends from work, fellow cafeteria ladies who seemed content to sip pale beer and watch former high school students fill the beer garden with their rowdy ways. Yes, Anna dug the Hairnets immensely. She liked the way they hunched their shoulders, smirking as they smoked menthol cigarettes from the communal packs piled in front of them. She'd had a few beers and twice called the Hairnets lunchroom heroes, holding up her red plastic cup to them in salute. She pitied her husband and his boring walkabout.

"You worried about something, honey?"

Anna drummed her fingernails against the side of her cup. It took her a second to realize that her in-law was speaking to her.

"What?"

"Your forehead's creased. You look worried."

Anna smiled. "No, I'm good."

"Tyler should be by any minute now," Bernie said, tapping her cigarette against the picnic table's overflowing ashtray. "He's just clearing his thoughts."

"I know, Bernie. Seriously. I'm fine."

The Hairnets nodded knowingly and sipped their beer. The country band had switched speeds and was now singing "Fishing in the Dark" by the Nitty Gritty Dirt Band. Couples stood up from the picnic tables around them and snaked toward the stage.

Anna got to her feet. "I'm going to get something to eat."

"Try the steak kabobs," Bernie said, stubbing out her cigarette. "I hear they're pretty good."

The crowd was thinner outside the beer garden. Mostly kids and their parents, sitting on the curb and eating corn dogs and grilled sweet corn and popcorn and anything else made out of corn. She passed the cotton candy vendor and the deep-fried doughnuts. The air smelled sweet. Almost grilled. She joined the steak kabob line. The kid ahead of her kept pulling up his baggy pants with one hand, clenching the jean fabric with one hand and really hiking it up. He had a wallet chain, and the chain dipped so low it almost touched the ground. Anna smirked at his outfit and then felt old for smirking, hopelessly out of touch. No one ever told her that at twenty-seven she'd feel so ancient.

She bought her steak kabob and ate it standing beneath a street lamp. A few mitters were flitting around the lamp's orange light, but they seemed sluggish from the heat and didn't make much of an effort to collide with anything. The sun had set, but the sky was still a bright shade of blue. A man in a cowboy hat walked through the crowd, stopping every five feet to chat with people. He noticed Anna beneath the street lamp and headed over. He touched the brim of his hat and smiled.

"Evening, Anna."

"Hi, Sheriff."

"You enjoying yourself?"

"Sure," Anna said, taking a bite of grilled steak. "Who doesn't love a street festival, right?"

"Now that's the God's honest," Merritt said, hitching his thumbs through his belt. "I remember coming to these things as a kid. I thought they were the mightiest thing going on in the whole world."

Anna bit into a piece of steak and dragged it down the end of the skewer. The meat was tough and spicy. "Say, I've been meaning to ask you something," Merritt said, swaying back on the heels of his cowboy boots. "Have you seen that chunk of meteorite Clyde Ringston got himself stabbed by?"

"No. Why?"

"Well, we had it go missing from the evidence locker recently. It would have been in a labeled plastic bag."

"Sorry, I haven't seen any rocks in plastic bags lately. Why are you asking me?"

"Just covering all my bases. I'm going to need to ask your husband, too."

"That's fine with me. Maybe you'll be able to get more sense out of him than I can these days."

Merritt nodded. He was still turned forward, watching the crowd. Anna wondered how well he could read her from the corner of his eye. She kept her face blank and nibbled on the steak kabob, although she'd already lost her appetite. Where was Tyler? How far was he walking?

Merritt pushed his hat off his forehead. "Ty's taking Clyde's death pretty rough."

"You could say that. He drinks too much and he hardly sleeps."

"Death is a hard thing when it gets that close to you. You can almost feel it brush up against your shoulder as it goes by for somebody else. I felt it in that farmhouse that afternoon, I can tell you that."

"I'm sure," Anna said, though at the moment she wasn't too sure about anything. Merritt Jackson's gray eyes had turned muddled, as if a fog bank had rolled across them and settled low on the ground. "You know," the sheriff said, "I worked on a cattle ranch in New Mexico when I was about Tyler's age. Being the youngest hand on the premises, I got all the shit jobs, like retrieving stock when it wandered off from the herd. One day in July, a steer disappeared. Nothing un-usual there. I went out after lunch thinking I could rope the steer in and get back before dinner. I rode around all the usual places, but I couldn't find that darn steer anywhere. A couple of hours went by and I started figuring this steer was more lost than others, so I rode harder and went out farther than usual, sort of circling around, widening the search. Eventually I rode through a narrow valley out in the middle of nothing. The valley was dried up, with no plants or animals, not even sagebrush. I kept riding, thinking that if the steer made it this far it must have been pretty tuckered by now.

"I was ready to turn and head back to the ranch when something glittered in the distance. I rode farther, until I could make out a trailer sitting all by itself. Now, I was a curious young man, and it seemed to me the reasonable thing to do would be to ride up to the trailer and introduce myself. Heck. Maybe they'd seen the steer and could help me out.

"The trailer was an old Airstream model, silver as a bullet. Its windows were shut and the yard around it was empty. No truck, no campfire, no clothes strung up on a line of rope. Not even a water pump, far as I could tell. It was like someone had picked the trailer up and dropped it in the valley, like you'd drop a hot potato wrapped in tinfoil. I couldn't find anywhere to tie my horse up, so I told it not to go anywhere and left it standing in the valley, blinking at all that nothing. I knocked on the trailer door, but nobody answered. I tried the doorknob. It was open. I shouted hello again and waited. Still no answer, so I went inside.

"I thought it'd be roasting inside that trailer, with the July heat and all, but it was cool, almost dank. I stood inside the doorway and let my eyes get used to the darkness. On my right was a bed, tucked against the wall, and in front of me was a sink and some cupboards. On my left was a booth for the kitchen table and a hallway running to the back of the trailer, where there must have been a bathroom and more sleeping compartments. It was the first trailer home I'd ever been inside of, and it was like stepping into a smaller world inside the regular world you were used to.

"I didn't particularly want to search the rear of the trailer, or go right back outside into the heat, so I sat down in the little kitchen booth and lay my head on the table. My head was pounding from the ride. I knew I'd have to turn back for the day and leave the steer to her fate. The boss wouldn't like it, but what could I do? Ride until my horse dropped out from under me? I took out my canteen and drank, dribbling some of the water over my forehead. Something shifted in the booth across from me and a man sat up, groaning. I about spit water, I was so surprised. He'd been lying there all along, only three feet between us.

"He was an old coot. Ninety years, easy. His face was tanned, wrinkled, and drawn up in a pucker, like the top of a pumpkin. His eyes swung around slow in their sockets, not really landing on anything for too long. He looked at me and kept on going. I waved my hand in front of his face. He mashed his lips together and frowned. 'So you found me out,' he said. 'I'm blind as a stone.'

" 'I'm sorry to hear that,' I told him. 'My name's Merritt Jackson.'

"'I don't care what your name is,' the old coot said. 'Do I look like I care what your name is?'

"'You don't look like much of anything.'

"His jaw dropped like he was going to belly-laugh, but no sound came out except this soft wheezing that made my toes curl inside my boots. I thought about sliding out of the booth right there and getting on home, but I stayed. I was still young enough to believe I'd be able to get some sense out of him.

"'You live out here by yourself, sir?'

"The old coot shook his head. 'You call this living? Shit, son. This isn't living. This is nothing but holding on. I haven't lived for years now.'

"'How about supplies? What do you do for food and water?'

"'They bring me what I need.'

"'Who does?'

"The old coot waved his hand like he was swatting off a gnat. 'The church in town drops it off. They've got a kid with a dirt bike. He likes to see how much sand he can churn up on the way back to town.'

"'What town is that?'

"'San Pecos.'

"'That's a good ten miles from here. You're telling me the kid rides twenty miles, off-road, to bring you beans and water?'

"'He's a good kid. He loves to ride.'

"The old man sneezed without covering his nose. I sat

back and looked out the trailer window. My horse was standing right where I'd left her, sniffing at the ground. It was all rock and soil, though, and she wasn't having much luck finding anything green to eat. We might as well have been in a space station on Mars. I wondered if coyotes came around at night, sniffing at the trailer for food. Anything roaming in the area would have been hungry enough to risk the smell of man.

" 'Don't you get lonely way out here?'

" 'No, I can't say I do. It's not loneliness if you hunt it out for yourself.'

" 'That doesn't make sense. Lonely is lonely.'

" 'I didn't say it would make sense to you, son. You're still young. You still chase women and money and booze, expecting they'll change something in you that can't be changed.'

" 'What's that?'

" 'That heart, right there in your chest. It's counting down with every tick.'

" 'Is that right, then? So will I be less alone when it stops ticking?'

" 'Oh, I wouldn't say that,' the old man said, and this time he did laugh out loud, wheezing and pounding the table with his fist. I got up from the table and went to the cupboards. I found a jug of water and filled my canteen up. He was still laughing when I went outside and shut the trailer door. You could hear him laughing in there, even with all the windows shut, and the sound must have spooked my horse because she'd already run off, headed in the general direction of home. I followed her on foot and didn't catch up with her until dusk. We camped next to a muddy excuse for a stream that night, instead of riding in the dark, and I didn't get back to the ranch until lunch the next day.

"And you know what? That damn steer had already found her own way home, the night before."

Merritt adjusted his belt. Anna blinked and looked around, wondering how long they'd been standing under the street lamp. The carnival crowd was still steadily flowing past, though fewer young children walked hand in hand with their parents, shouting and pointing at things. The country band had taken a break and departed the beer garden stage to drink along with everyone else.

"Why'd you tell me that story, Sheriff?"

Merritt sighed. "I don't know. Sometimes I just go on like that. Mouth like a train with no brakes."

"Did you ever see the old man again?"

"No, ma'am. I was out that way a couple more times, but I couldn't seem to find the right canyon."

"You couldn't find him again? Ever? That's pretty messed up."

Merritt shrugged. "I don't know about that. There've been a few days when I felt like heading for the desert myself."

A cloud of incandescent white light rose in Anna's mind. She could hear the rattle of thin windows in thin metal frames and the methodic thump of something big approaching. Shock and awe. Sodom and Gomorrah. Melted, gaping faces stared at each other in surprise as the cities around them went up in curls of smoke.

"Sure," she said. "I can see that."

TWENTY-SEVEN

The house was quiet. Roscoe slept on the couch and Tyler stepped softly, not wanting to wake the dog and deal with an exuberant welcome home. He went into the dark kitchen, felt for a light switch, and flipped it on. The white linoleum tiles glowed, the aluminum toaster gleamed, and the entire kitchen appeared impossibly clean and artificial after a day of walking across mountain and desert. The oven's digital clock said it was 8:36. He'd been gone for hours.

Tyler opened a cupboard door and took out an empty Mason jar. He filled the jar with water and drank it back to empty while standing in front of the sink. The water fattened his tongue and inflated the lining of his desiccated cheeks. He felt dizzy. He filled the Mason jar a second time and set it on the counter. The tap water was running at its coldest now. Tyler dipped his entire head beneath the water, shuddering at the sudden chill. He thought of the spaceship hovering silently above the copper pit, blowing cold air into the desert.

Maybe it used liquid nitrogen as a cooling mechanism. It probably had some sort of nuclear (or hypernuclear) engine, something that ran hot and needed a powerful coolant to counteract the engine's intense temperature. Sure. That made sense.

Tyler pulled his head out and turned off the water. He dried his face and hair with a dishtowel. Roscoe watched him from the doorway, head cocked. "Hey, buddy. How's it going?" Roscoe barked, but stayed in the doorway. Tyler held out his hand and let the dog sniff it. He left the kitchen without turning the light off and went back into the living room, trailed by Roscoe. He sat in the second pea-green recliner, opposite Bernie's. He set the water jar on an end table and kicked the footrest out. He considered his dusty shoes. The dog barked. "They're all downtown tonight," Tyler told him, smoothing out the fur on the dog's head. Roscoe whined and poked his snout into Tyler's kneecap. Tyler pushed the dog away. Roscoe turned and stared at the door. Tyler sat up. "Okay, okay." He slid out of the recliner without collapsing the footrest, his legs and back stiff. He opened the door to the front hall and Roscoe surged past him. Tyler pushed the dog aside and opened the outer door.

"Be free, Roscoe. Be free."

The dog stood on the edge of the doorway and looked at Tyler.

"What?"

Roscoe barked.

"Go! Go outside."

Roscoe sat down and thumped the hall floor with his tail. Tyler groaned. "Let me guess. You want to go see Bernie and Anna."

Roscoe barked again. The phone rang inside the house. "Give me a minute," Tyler told the dog, closing the outer door. "We'll see."

The nearest phone was on a table between the couch and Bernie's chair. Tyler sat on the couch and picked up the receiver. "Hello?"

"Tyler? Is that you?"

"Hi, Mom."

"Am I calling too late? What time is it there?"

"No, it's good. We're two hours behind Omaha, not ahead. Hey. It must be pretty late there."

"Oh, you know us. We're two old night owls. Your father is working on one of his puzzles. He's got one that's the entire New York City skyline at sunset. I'm excited to see how it turns out."

"He's still doing those?"

"Sure is. He likes to keep busy. How's Anna?"

"She's been having nightmares. She wants to move home."

"Now, there's nothing wrong with that. I've had a bad feeling about this from the day you told me you wanted to move."

"Mom. Please."

"What? I can speak my mind, can't I? It's a free country."

"I need the job. We need to save money."

"You can't work here? Your father could get you a job at the plant just by picking up the phone. A nice office job with your own desk and a computer."

"We've gone over this. I didn't want to live in Nebraska for my whole life."

"Okay, so you've proved your point."

"What?"

"You've lived in Nevada. Now you can come home."

"It's only been three months."

"A lot can happen in three months, honey."

Tyler didn't know what to say to that. She was right.

"Anyhow. How's my sister?"

"Bernie's good."

"Does she still smoke like a chimney?"

"Yeah. She smokes."

"I never could understand how she could move out west like that. Who wants to live in the middle of the desert?"

"It's beautiful here. I've joined an astronomy club."

His mother sighed on the other end of the line. "I saw a boy the other day. He looked like Cory."

"You did?"

"He was at the grocery store."

"You didn't go up to him, did you?"

His mother didn't say anything. Tyler could hear his father shouting in the background, asking his mother if they had any popcorn left.

"Mom?"

"I had to know. I had to ask him. He looked just like him, but his hair was different. His bangs were longer."

"Oh god."

"I told him the whole story. He was very understanding. He even said he'd keep an eye out and let me know if he saw anything. I gave him one of your father's old business cards with his cell phone number on it."

Tyler set the phone down in his lap. Roscoe was lying in the front hall doorway, panting as he watched Tyler talk on the phone. Tyler took a deep breath and brought the phone back to his mouth.

"Mom, you can't keep doing that. It's time to let it go."

"I know."

"Do you?"

"Yes. No. I don't know."

"He's gone. He's not coming back."

"You don't know that. You can't say that for certain."

"It's been fifteen years. If Cody was going to come home, he would have done it by now."

"He might have been kidnapped. He might be waiting to make his escape."

"Not for fifteen years, Mom."

"Stranger things have happened."

"Not much stranger."

His mother didn't say anything for a minute. Tyler waited, wishing he'd never answered the phone. Roscoe was right. It was time to go downtown. To get out of this silent house and join everyone at the beer garden. He'd grab some food, too. He hadn't eaten lunch. He was starving.

"Your father," his mother said, whispering.

"What about him?"

"He's started drinking again."

"Beer?"

"No," his mother said, still whispering. "He thinks I can't smell it, but I can. I don't care what anybody says. Vodka has a smell."

"You should tell him to call his sponsor."

"He won't. He doesn't care. He doesn't care about anything anymore."

"That's not true. He cares about you. He loves you, Mom."

"Not as much as he loves vodka, apparently."

Tyler stood up from the couch. "I have to go."

"Alright."

"I love you."

"I know, Tyler."

"Put the screws on Dad. Call his sponsor yourself if you have to."

"Okay. I will. Say hello to Anna for me. Tell her I hope she stops having those nightmares."

"Sure thing. Bye."

Tyler hung up the phone. Roscoe stood up in the entryway and wagged his tail. Tyler picked the water jar off the end table and drank with his eyes closed. His stomach sloshed as he set the jar down and started across the living room. One of

Roscoe's enormous rubber chew bones was lying on the floor, slick with saliva, and Tyler didn't notice the chew toy until he slipped on it and fell forward. He stuck his arms out and caught himself on the hulking TV set. The impact jarred the TV and the framed picture of Leonard Nemoy flew into the wall and bounced to the floor. Tyler picked up the picture. The glass was broken, and the signed photograph had a gash running down its middle.

"Damn, Spock. I'm sorry." Tyler laid the picture on top of the TV. He grabbed a nylon windbreaker off a hook in the front hall and went outside, Roscoe charging ahead down the front steps and into the rocky garden. Tyler thought about grabbing a leash for the dog, but he was tired of being dragged around. He opened the gate. The dog bounded off into the night, heading downtown toward all the good smells. Tyler latched the gate and followed the dog, scanning the shadowed front yards for movement. The neighborhood was quiet. Tonight the party was downtown.

TWENTY-EIGHT

Merritt Jackson excused himself and left Anna standing beneath the street lamp. She didn't know what his weird story about the old man in the Airstream trailer was supposed to mean, but it had made her nervous. Jackson spoke slowly, but he was a canny old dude. He'd been dealing with liars his whole life and, sure enough, he'd pegged her falseness, even with the beauty queen smile.

"Anna?"

Tyler stepped out of the crowd. Even in the orange light, you could tell he was sunburned.

"Where have you been?"

"I just got back into town. I went for a walk in the mountains."

"In the mountains?"

"It was beautiful."

"Did you try to avoid every spot of shade, or what? You're

going to peel for a week, Mountain Man. I wouldn't be surprised if you had sunstroke." A little boy and a girl ran past in the crowd, screaming as they chased each other. A balding father trudged after them, not bothering to shout warnings as he drank his beer. Anna slapped her sides. "Anyhow. Let's go on a ride, Ty. Let's go on the Ferris wheel."

"Sounds good to me."

Tyler bought two tickets and they got in line for the ride. The night was still warm, but a cool breeze had started to blow through Main Street, floating Styrofoam cups and greasy plastic wrappers into the air like trashy ghosts. Dust flew into the mouths of the children standing in line, making them spit onto the street as they hopped from foot to foot, buzzing with too much sugar, too fast. The Ferris wheel was lined with soft, blue lights. It turned slowly, each gondola filled with the inky outlines of its riders, their torsos hidden by the latched doors that kept them from falling to the earth.

The wheel slowed and its operator stepped up, halting the gondola nearest to the ground. He unlatched the door and a teenage couple stepped out. Two others came forward and took the couple's place. The operator stepped back and the wheel continued turning until the next gondola reached the ground, and the whole loading-unloading process was repeated again. It went on this way, with the cool breeze rising and falling, until their turn came and the operator set them inside their own gondola, dropping the lap bar and telling them to watch their feet and hands before he slammed the door shut and threw the locking bolt. Anna set her hands in her lap as they rose into the sky and the wheel began to turn faster, fully loaded with new passengers.

Tyler put his arm around her. The mountains to the west were a lumpy outline in the darkness. The first stars had come out and Mars stood right above the horizon, a bright speck of reddish orange. Three different sets of blinking lights sailed west: more airplanes heading for California or down to Las Vegas for the weekend. Anyplace but central Nevada.

"Did you think about what I said about moving back to Nebraska?"

Tyler shifted under the lap bar. Anna could feel the heat of his body radiating through his windbreaker.

"I saw the alien again. He was up in the mountains."

"What alien?"

"The one I saw in the backyard. And on the Fourth of July."

"I don't know what you're talking about."

"I told you about it the night we had sex in the crater. We'd been drinking rum and Cokes."

Anna dropped her head against the seat. She recalled sitting with Mr. Diaz at the fall site. Tyler had made some stupid joke about aliens from outer space, and she'd told him he was full of crap.

"You were serious about that?"

"I saw what I saw."

"Ty, that's not healthy. Hallucinations are usually the sign of a much larger psychological problem."

"This time I saw his spaceship, too. It was silver and shaped like a saucer, just like you'd think."

Anna slid to the far edge of the gondola to get a better look at her husband. He wasn't smiling. He was staring straight ahead as the Ferris wheel turned and dipped them toward the ground. The machine's lights made his sunburned skin glow blue, as if he were verging on becoming an alien himself. "At first, you couldn't see anything but a mining pit," he continued, "but then it rose up out of the ground, like a submarine breeching the surface of the ocean. It went straight up in the air and stopped in front of me. It was soundless."

The Ferris wheel had swung around again. Their gondola rose higher, almost near the top. The wind blew through them, definitely cold now. Anna breathed into her hands. This ride had been a bad idea.

"The ship stopped and the alien came out. He stood on the deck of the ship. I spoke to him, but he didn't say anything back. His eyes were so old, Anna. They looked like they'd seen a thousand years, at least. I think he was trying to communicate with his mind, but I was so unadvanced I couldn't pick up anything. I settled for throwing a rock at it. I might as well have been a monkey."

Anna shivered and rubbed her arms. The sky had gone from a dark blue to a deep black. Even from this height, she couldn't see any city lights beyond Wormwood. Silverton might as well have been on the other side of the planet.

Tyler drummed his hands on the lap bar. "You don't believe me, do you?"

"I don't know."

"Does everything have to be so practical with you? Does everything have to make sense?"

"Ty, there aren't any aliens from outer space. You've been reading too much science fiction, smoking too much pot, and you've gone off your rocker. Heck, I don't blame you. This place would make anybody start seeing spaceships. That's why we need to leave, Ty. This isn't our home."

"Bernie will believe me. She's believes in aliens. We're in a whole group that believes in them."

"You mean your nerdy astronomy club?"

"Their planet is lush and green. They're very advanced. They're going to save us from ourselves."

"God," Anna said, examining her nails. "Give me a break, Ty."

The Ferris wheel halted to let out passengers. Their gondola hung swinging, still high in the air. Anna's stomach fluttered and she gripped the lap bar with both hands. The ground seemed to roll under them, like someone shaking out a carpet. Tyler dropped his chin against his chest. The wheel's enormous, unseen engine whined and the wheel began turning again, rotating to let the next set of passengers out. This time when the wheel stopped Anna was ready, her elbows locked against the lurching tug of gravity. The gondola swung under her, and Anna imagined what it would feel like to fall so far. She'd once been so beautiful that she could actually feel it, a force of pure energy that crackled with as much power and joy as any one human being could stand. She'd won awards. Accolades. And now here she was, growing old and wizened in the middle of the desert.

"My life's meaningless, isn't it, Tyler?"

"No one's life is meaningless."

"You guys could be totally right about the aliens."

"Who knows? I don't even know. Aliens are strange. Their customs are not our customs."

"God. I'm such a snobby bitch."

"Don't worry about it. Everyone's a snobby bitch."

Anna laughed and dried her eyes with her shirtsleeve. "You're such a dork, Tyler." Tyler pulled her against him as the wheel rotated down another notch. It was almost their turn to get off.

They stood in the Ferris wheel's blue shadow, wobbling unsteadily as they got their land legs back. The crowd had thinned out and the rides were going dark, though the beer garden was still packed with people. Six lines of people stood in front of the portable toilets, chatting with each other. Anna set her hand on her husband's shoulder and picked a pebble out of her shoe. "If we're staying in Wormwood," she said, "I think I need to drink some more beer."

"That sounds awesome. And I'm starving."

Anna straightened up and looked around. The food court was dark. The metal window doors on each trailer closed and padlocked.

"Ah, I think all the food vendors have gone home for the night. But Taco Thunder is still open."

"Really?"

"Bernie told me the Diaz family keeps it open every year until the beer garden closes down. They make a killing."

"I think I'll have to take a detour before I join you in the garden. Tell Bernie to save a dance for me."

"Okay. See you later."

Anna tugged at her paper beer garden bracelet and watched as Tyler crossed Main Street and disappeared behind Mr. Diaz's shack. She liked how Tyler stood up straight as he walked, always watching the area around him. She liked that about her husband. It was optimistic.

TWENTY-NINE

Mr. Diaz watched Tyler cross the parking lot. His white suit reflected light from the street lamps, reverberating in a funky shade of burnt ocher that was hard to look at. Taco Thunder shone brightly behind him as people went in and out of the restaurant, dangling plastic bags filled with beef burritos and soft-shell tacos from their fingertips. The sweet fried cinnamon *churros* drifted over to Tyler. He licked his lips.

"Evening, Mr. Diaz." Diaz nodded in reply, but didn't speak. Tyler continued toward the buzzing Mexican restaurant, kicking aside broken chunks of asphalt as he went. He pulled open the restaurant's exterior door and stepped inside the entryway. Through the glass interior doors he could see couples sitting in red vinyl booths drinking strawberry margaritas. He opened the second door and stood inside the restaurant. About half the booths were full, and a family of four sat at a table in the middle of the room, sharing an enormous plate of super nachos. The hostess station was deserted for the moment. He could hear Rosa Diaz in the back of the restaurant, speaking rapid-fire Spanish to someone in the kitchen. He wondered if he should wait for her to come out, or if he could just seat himself.

"Mr. Mayfield."

Tyler turned to his left. Skull and his girlfriend, Bratt, smiled at him from a booth. "You picking up carryout?"

"No," Tyler said. "I'm here to eat."

Skull slid over in the booth. "You want to eat with us?"

"Really?"

"Totally," Bratt said, smiling. "Have a seat."

"But I'm a teacher. Aren't you worried about being cool?"

"No," Skull said, "we're really not."

Tyler sat down. Bratt reached across the table and handed him a paper menu. He settled on chicken fajitas with a side of tamales. The teens ate red and blue chips from a wicker bowl. Angela Diaz appeared at their table with an extra glass of water and took everyone's order. Tyler tried not to stare at the metal studs in Bratt's nose or the silver rings that ran along the cartilage ridges in her ears. He remembered the backseat of Skull's car, the gleaming flecks of metal and pale flesh. He drank his water. Bratt was watching him.

"Looks like you got some sun today, Mr. Mayfield."

"Yeah," Skull said. "When you first came in, we thought you were some sort of half-man, half-lobster."

"I wish. I always loved that one huge claw they had."

The teenagers laughed. A couple got up from their table and left the restaurant. The air-conditioning kicked in as the waitress appeared with their food. Tyler dug into his fajitas and the ache in his stomach slowly departed. He found himself thinking about his mother and father, alone in Omaha. His father, sitting for hours hunched over the dining room table, sneaking pulls of vodka as he put his puzzles together. His mother watching public television in the living room, knitting the scarves she donated to their church every December. He could picture each of them, in their separate rooms, looking up every time a door slammed in their neighborhood, or a car pulled into someone else's driveway.

Would he share a fate like theirs? No matter where he lived?

"What do you think, Tyler?"

Tyler set his fork down. He'd already finished his chicken fajitas, but the two large, deep-fried tamales were still untouched. He belched into his napkin and wiped the grease from his lips.

"Think about what?"

Bratt pushed around a pile of yellow rice on her plate. "How long do you think until the end of the world?"

"I think," Tyler said, "the world will go on long enough. Not too short, but not too long, either."

"Long enough for what?"

"Pain," Tyler said, picking up his fork again. "Long enough for just enough pain to occur, and when the world's had enough, it'll cease to exist."

"That's pretty dark, man," Skull said. "Even for an English teacher."

Tyler pushed the main plate away and set the side plate in front of him. He cut off a chunk of tamale with the side of his fork. Exposed, the diced meat and crushed peppers inside the fried cornmeal shell steamed in the open air. Tyler looked around the room as he ate the tamales. The family of four had finished eating and had left the restaurant. Taco Thunder was clearing out. It was getting late, and Anna would be waiting for him.

Tyler slid out of the booth. "Okay," he said, "I'm going to the bathroom. You two kids figure out the world while I'm gone."

"Sure, Mr. Mayfield. No problem."

Tyler made his way down a long hallway decorated with paintings of bulls, bullfighters, and bullfighting arenas. He caught a lot of golden sequins and flowing red capes in the corner of his vision as he went along, humming to himself. He felt a little high, as if the weed he'd smoked earlier had returned to give him a boost.

The bathroom was at the end of the hall. It had a urinal and a toilet and smelled like pine-scented antiseptic mixed with roasted corn tortillas. The soles of Tyler's shoes slid across the greasy floor tiles. He saw himself in the mirror and flinched. His sunburn had grown worse somehow. He'd basically turned into a walking neon pink highlighter.

Tyler splashed water on his face. Pipes groaned and rattled inside the wall behind the sink. He turned off the water, but the pipes didn't stop rattling. Tyler pounded on the wall. The pipes moaned, then squealed as if they'd been stretched apart. The vanity mirror began shaking and swung open, revealing four dusty glass shelves. Tyler stepped back. It wasn't just the mirror and the sink: The entire bathroom was vibrating.

"Shit."

The knob on the bathroom door rattled, as if angry and alive. Tyler grabbed it and pulled the door open. He stood in the doorway and looked down the long hallway toward the front of the restaurant. Something heavy crashed on the other side of the wall, in the kitchen. A man shouted, his voice unintelligible. Tyler thought about running down the hallway and rejoining the others, but the ground had begun to roll, funhouse style, and he decided to stay where he was.

A white insulation panel dropped from the ceiling to the hallway floor. A second panel fell, and then a third. The lights went out. Something big fell on the other side of the wall, shattering loudly. Tyler imagined a hundred porcelain dishes and cups lying in fragments on the kitchen floor. The ceiling shuddered. Wooden beams snapped, sounding like gunshots. A man screamed from the front of the restaurant. Tyler gripped the doorway's trim, digging his nails into the cheap wood. The ceiling buckled inward, folding like an accordion, and plaster dust rained down, coating everything.

The shaking grew worse, then stopped.

Tyler heard a woman in the front of the restaurant ask if it was over. He was about to let go of the door frame and step forward when the roof fell in with a thump, throwing him backward.

THIRTY

The band had stopped playing, but no one in the beer garden seemed to care or even notice. The Hairnets had called it quits for the night and Anna and Bernie sat alone at their picnic table, watching the crowd as they drank their beer and drifted along their own currents of thought, smoke rising from Bernie's cigarettes and into the sky. Anna felt good. She had the day off tomorrow, and this was her fifth beer.

"I think I need to use the ladies' room," Anna said, rising to her feet. "How about you, Bernie?"

"No, thank you, dear. I think I'll hold the fort down."

"You're an angel, Bernie."

"I don't know about that."

"Well, you are. Letting us stay in your house and eat your food."

"It's been a pleasure having you," Bernie said, smiling. "It's nice to have noise in the house for once that isn't just the wind."

Anna gave her in-law a drunken curtsy and entered the moving crowd. She wove her way outside the orange fence and got in line to use the portapotties. Most of the people in line were thin, tanorexic women with big hair and denim jackets. Anna dug her cell phone out of her pocket to see if anyone had called. No one had called. She slid the phone back in her pocket and fingered the paper bracelet on her wrist.

Beneath her feet, the earth began to move.

The earthquake was hard to process at first. Anna was from the Midwest, where tornadoes were the thing. Massive funnels of dirty, black wind ripping through cornfields, silos, and trailer parks always set on the exposed side of town. In Nebraska, the sky could be clear and sunny one minute and clouded the next, an unnatural quasi sunlight filtering down from above, giving everything a surreal, lemon-yellow tint. The air could swirl in on itself until it thickened into a funnel, and that funnel spun toward you, its path as unpredictable as an angry drunk's.

But this was different. This was a force of nature rising up from below, moving the ground itself. Nothing was reliable anymore. You couldn't duck into a house or run into the basement. In fact, every structure now posed a threat to you. Buildings could teeter and collapse at any moment, burying you in rubble, crushing your fragile body, your soft skull.

The women in the bathroom line staggered as the ground shifted. They looked at one another, drunk and incredulous. A woman burst out of one of the toilets, slamming the plastic door behind her as she staggered out with her jeans and underwear still around her ankles. The women in line watched her go past and finally trip on her own pants, sprawling into the dirt with her scrawny bare ass in the air. This should have been funny, Anna thought, but it wasn't. The ground was shaking. The portable toilets knocked against one another and made a dull thudding sound, and one woman screamed and then another, and Anna thought she could hear the wastewater sloshing inside the toilets. A man wearing a green baseball cap burst out of another stall, trying to fasten his belt as he jumped out. He must have been really drunk, because he looked at the screaming women like he didn't know what they were screaming about. He shouted at everyone and staggered forward, laughing.

Anna turned from the toilets and began to run, but stopped again when she couldn't decide which direction to go. The street lamps flickered, and each time natural objects appeared in new and surprising places. The vendor carts crept closer. Fences drew back. Even the street lamps themselves were unreliable, popping up in spots Anna was certain no lamp had been before.

The quake rode up through her feet, ankles, and calves. It swung into her hips, and when she tried to walk, it was like walking on a waterbed. She saw a boy riding a bike. The boy fought with the bike's handlebars, as if the bike itself was trying to change their destination. The boy rode right into a storefront window, pitched forward over the handlebars, and crashed through the glass. Anna called for help, but she was standing alone on an empty patch of street. The boy popped up inside the store and leapt back out through the window. The building trembled behind him, hungry. The boy had blood on his face, arms, and hands. He looked at Anna, paused, and bolted down the street, leaving his bike lying in a patch of broken glass. Anna thought of her husband. He was on the other end of Main Street. He was in this earthquake, too.

It couldn't have been long, maybe thirty seconds, since the earth started to shake, but time had turned to syrup and Anna had to wade through it. She wanted to find her husband and make sure he was alright, but the Ferris wheel had begun to rock back and forth and it's creaking frame hypnotized her. While the street lamps flickered on and off, the Ferris wheel actually lit up again, regaining its blue-green glow, and the longer it swayed the more certain she felt it was going to fall.

Even the earthquake hadn't sobered up the crowd. They stepped closer to the swaying Ferris wheel, entranced by the blue glow, the movement. They smiled as they watched, their eyes filled with light. They still held red plastic beer cups in their hands. They'd come for a show.

The blue-green light and the swaying, thickly blurred lines it made against the night sky was beautiful, so beautiful, but Anna felt an itching at the back of her mind, a certainty that had been drilled into her over the past few months of nightmares: yes. This sort of sluggish, destructive beauty was dangerous, and had to be dealt with accordingly. She lowered her eyes. She rubbed her flushed face until her mind cleared and she could think. All these idiots were going to be killed. That wheel would fall, and their soft skulls would all be crushed.

Anna went up to the biggest, fattest man in the crowd and threw her beer in his face. He blinked and looked at her as the beer dripped down his beard and onto his black motorcycle jacket.

"When that thing falls, it's going to fall on us. Do you understand? It will kill everybody standing here."

The big man touched the side of his beer-drenched face. After another long second, the big man's eyes cleared and he began to move, bellowing at the crowd. Anna bellowed along with him. They herded the crowd down the street, screaming movement into their bones, shoving sense into them. The ground shook harder and people lost their footing and fell only to be hauled up again by the people behind them. Above all the noise, the metal wheel moaned as it swung back and forth, like something deeply unhappy, but Anna didn't pause to look back. She heard a screeching, thunderous crash and kept running. A brick flew past her head. She dove to the ground and slid on the asphalt street and blood pounded in her ears like a steady, foot-stomping ovation.

The Ferris wheel's blue lights had gone out.

The ground had stopped moving.

THIRTY-ONE

Tyler Mayfield lay in a pocket of space and waited to either be crushed or rescued. Something heavy had pinned him. He could see a patch of stars through a gap in the rubble. He felt cold, but wasn't in any pain. No pain at all. He could smell cooked meat and flour tortillas, buried somewhere nearby. He shouted for help, but his voice sounded tinny in his ears. It was hard to imagine anyone hearing that.

After the letting-go ceremony, his parents gave Tyler the job of boxing up his brother's things so they could turn Cody's bedroom into a study. Tyler put the job off for months. No one rushed him. Spiders had taken the room over, spinning complex webs that resembled silvery afghans too beautiful to be worn. Everything was coated with dust. Posters lost their adhesion and curled off the walls, one by one.

One day Tyler finally went into his older brother's room. He dropped a dozen boxes in the middle of the floor, popped the windows open, and left again. He returned a few hours later wearing yellow scrub gloves. He went through his brother's collection of tape cassettes and CDs and dropped it all into a box. He did the same thing with the avalanche of papers on his brother's desk, untouched since his mother had rifled through them in the first days after Cody's disappearance. He boxed up the books, the magazines, and the white athletic socks. He created cardboard box towers, and gradually a cardboard city rose up in the center of the room. He worked around the city, adding to it, stacking box on top of box until the towers began to lean to the side as he walked past them. The posters curled willingly into thin, waxy tubes. He stuffed one tube inside another until they'd formed a single, thick roll that felt heavy in your hand and made you want to smack something.

Tyler hauled the boxes to the basement, where he started a new cardboard city in a room even more dank and cobwebbed than the one upstairs. No one else was home. He had the house to himself. He felt like a janitor working in the basement of a two-hundred-story skyscraper on Christmas Eve. After Tyler brought the last box down, he sat down on the basement's concrete floor and drew his knees to his chest. He leaned back against the block wall and stared at the cardboard towers and wondered if this was where his brother lived now, inside this cardboard city. Perhaps, somehow, Cody had shrunk to the size of a dust particle, too small to shout for help, and now his older brother wandered inside these boxes, lost in the maze of cardboard streets.

Tyler thought about saying something, in case his brother was here with him, in the basement, but he kept his mouth shut. He didn't want to scare Cody with his thunderous giant's voice and make him run any farther than he already had.

The rubble shifted and pressed against Tyler's chest. It was getting hard to breathe. He could still see the stars through the gap and they floated in his vision like fireflies.

"Hello? Anybody there?"

He could hear sirens in the distance. Fire trucks and ambulances. He wondered if anything was actually on fire. He couldn't smell smoke, but that didn't mean anything. The dust from the broken Sheetrock and torn insulation had plugged his nose. The whole world could have been on fire.

A light swept across Tyler's face. He thought of the alien and was glad it had returned to rescue him. He'd go with it. They'd travel across the distant regions of space, neither of them speaking to the other for twenty, thirty years, until the day came they grew so lonely and so bored they had to sit down together, at a table, and begin to speak out loud. The alien would tell of its ancient home world, now shattered and drifting, its remains caught in some back-alley asteroid belt somewhere. The alien would speak of epic wars, great loves, and bright accomplishments of talent, grace, and beauty. The alien would talk about millions of years of history, of the generations who lived and died on his planet, and, of course, now the alien was the last of its kind, and when it died so would all these stories. The alien's eyes would pour out sadness in waves as it spoke, filling the entire ship with a palpable sense of desolation, and he'd be able to hear the engine humming low, a dense ball of heat wrapped in layers of cold. After the alien finished with this magnificent history, with so many years lost and nearly forgotten, Tyler would speak of his own pains, and the alien would understand him perfectly.

The sweeping light returned.

"Mr. Mayfield, is that you?"

The rubble shifted above him and grew lighter. He was able to move his arms. He squinted into the light.

"Skull?"

"Don't worry, man. We'll get you out."

"Thank you. I'd appreciate that."

Skull and Bratt pulled him out of the rubble. Others had stumbled out as well and called to one another in the dark. The restaurant's roof had fallen in a sharp V, creating a pair of enormous lean-tos where a single open space had been an hour before. The light from Skull's cell phone revealed enough wreckage to allow them to weave their way safely out of the restaurant and back into the parking lot. The street lamps had gone out totally. A man rode toward them on horseback.

"You folks alright?"

"Hey, Sheriff," Bratt said. "We're okay."

Merritt slid off his horse and dropped to the ground. He scratched beneath the brim of his hat. "Can you believe this? An earthquake. We haven't had an earthquake in thirty years."

"It's pretty sick," Skull said. "We were in Taco Thunder and the roof fell in."

"The whole roof?"

"Pretty much."

"Shoot," Merritt said. "The Ferris wheel fell over, if you can believe that. Landed right on top of the hardware store."

"Holy shit. The hardware store?"

Tyler felt along his arms and legs for any breaks. He still wasn't completely sure he was alive. "Anybody hurt, Merritt?"

"A few cuts and bruises, but nothing major's been reported yet. As far as I can tell, Taco Thunder's the only building that flat-out collapsed. You know, I'm not entirely certain that Charles Diaz paid top dollar when he had the building built. He has a way of skimping on things like that."

Merritt left them to go check on the other restaurant survivors. Tyler could make out Rosa Diaz's voice, shouting something about the Richter scale and property insurance. Sirens wailed in the distance. When he looked down the street, Tyler could see dark clumps of people standing in circles, just like them. The plastic fence that ran around the beer garden had fallen over. A man was sitting on top of one of the picnic tables by himself, smoking a cigarette. A woman leapt over the fallen fence and sprinted in their direction. She crossed the distance quickly and slammed into Tyler, almost knocking him down.

"Anna."

She hugged him hard as he lifted her up. "You're okay."

"Yes, I—"

"You're okay."

"I am."

"God, Ty."

"I know."

"The Ferris wheel fell over. I shoved all these people out of the way. They were hypnotized."

"That's amazing."

She hugged him harder. "You're okay."

"We all are. You can relax."

Tyler set Anna back on the ground. She drew back to look at him, keeping her arms looped around his waist.

"You're all dirty."

"Taco Thunder's roof fell in. It's just plaster dust and dirt."

Anna licked her thumb and rubbed away the dirt around his eyes. Tyler glanced at Skull and Bratt, who were doing their best to look the other way. Behind them, the restaurant's parking lot was strangely empty.

"Hey. Where's the shelter?"

THIRTY-TWO

They found Roscoe at the edge of a fissure in the ground, pawing at the loose rock and soil. Both the shack and the meteorite had disappeared, as well as Mr. Diaz, and in their place was a strip of darkness about ten feet long and six feet across. Skull and Bratt went to get the sheriff while Anna and Tyler remained behind with the dog. "Roscoe," Tyler said, "you're not going to find him."

The dog continued pawing the ground, furry head low as he tried to pick up the lost scent. Anna stepped to the fissure's edge. She called Mr. Diaz's name, but the only answer she received was a cold updraft of wind. She shouted again, bending over the void until Tyler pulled her back. Anna couldn't believe it. The meteorite was gone. Mr. Diaz was gone. All that well-meant prophecy, and the apocalypse had come upon him, and him alone.

The town gathered in the parking lot. Most didn't even know about the fissure, had just assumed that this was where everyone would meet to talk about the earthquake. Sheriff Jackson and his deputies cordoned off the fissure with sawhorses and strips of yellow barricade tape. The Diaz women sat slumped in three metal folding chairs, wrapped in fireman blankets. Power had been restored to the street lamps and Anna could see people crying. A rescue attempt had been made to retrieve Diaz, but an aftershock had rippled through town right as they lowered a man down in a harness, halting the entire operation.

Not that it mattered, Anna thought. They wouldn't find him. That opening was too deep. It probably went on forever.

"Tyler, let's go—"

A woman shrieked. A ripple went through the crowd as some pushed forward to look into the fissure and others dropped back. Bernie had Roscoe by the collar, but the dog lunged against her grip, barking furiously. Someone else screamed, and now the entire crowd fell back, shouting. Anna and Tyler pushed against the crowd, toward the fissure. Everyone shouted at once. A fresh updraft of wind blew into the air, carrying the smell of fermented apples. Anna felt a light, rising sensation, as if she were drifting above her body.

"What is it, Tyler?"

"I don't know. I can't see."

The folks on the other side of the fissure could see. They

tripped over one another as they scrambled away, stopping a good twenty feet distant. The only person still near the fissure was a blond, wide-eyed little boy, sucking on his index finger as he watched. Anna leaned over the fissure and looked down. The rising feeling grew stronger as she saw a pale hand flash out of the darkness, grabbing onto a rock. A pale shape was attached to the hand.

"There's someone down there, Ty. They're trying to pull themselves up."

"Mr. Diaz?"

A second hand appeared and joined the first. A woman ran forward and swooped the little boy into her arms. She ran back from the fissure, ducking her head as if she were being shot at. The pale form pulled itself up and peered at Anna, dark-eyed, its ghostly jaw pulled long, like stretched taffy.

"No," Anna said, "not Mr. Diaz."

The pale form kept climbing, moving steadily from rock to rock, spiderlike in its agility. It had two arms and two legs, like a person, but its limbs were long, much longer than a human being's, and its hairless head was shaped like a balloon. A woman screamed as one of its hands let go of the rock and its entire body dipped backward, clinging to the fissure wall with only one arm as it peered into the abyss. When it swung its head around again it looked directly at Anna, who felt as if she'd fully risen from her body and was now drifting, weightless, somewhere in the glowing night sky.

"Wow," Tyler said. "This must be his cousin."

"Whose cousin?"

"The Visitor I saw in the mountains. He had eyes like that."

The alien continued climbing. It was only ten feet away now, on their side of the fissure. Its eyes were shaped like seeds, Anna realized. Watermelon seeds. And it didn't have a nose or ears. "Alien Crashes in Utah: Immediately Converts to Mormonism."

Tyler grabbed her hand and pulled her back for the second time that night. "We better give it space, Anna." Anna allowed herself to be pulled. Most of her was drifting far above, anyway, watching the event unfold like birds must watch events. The tiny people were screaming and shouting as the pale figure climbed steadily, unhurried, and the tiny dog barked and foamed as it tried to break free of its owner's grasp. The smell of dead apples rotting in the sun grew stronger and the tiny people put their hands over their noses, trying to block the smell. And the pale figure pulled itself out of the darkness, rising above them like a forgotten god.

The dog stopped barking and the crowd fell silent. The Visitor, well over seven feet tall, turned and took in the entire group. It kept its long, three-fingered hands at its sides, each finger tapered like the end of a candle and tipped with round, soft-looking pads. The wind had died down, and the rotten apple smell was stronger than ever. Tyler Mayfield, badly sunburned and coated with plaster dust, waited along with everyone else for the alien to speak, for it to ask to be taken to their leader. On the opposite side of the fissure, Felix Hill emerged from the crowd and stepped forward. "Greetings. We are so honored to have you here in Wormwood." The alien ignored the head of the Visitation Society and peered into the fissure. Felix followed the alien's gaze and his mouth dropped into a small, silent O. He looked up, eyes wide, and spoke across the open space directly to Tyler, as if they were alone in a small room. "My Lord, Tyler. There's more of them."

The crowd rippled. A man bolted away from the crowd, and then a couple of others followed. Tyler stepped forward and stood beside the alien. More pale, elongated shapes, ghostly white in the starlight, dotted the fissure on both sides, climbing with steady agility. They ascended with heads up-turned, their dark eyes focused on the fissure's opening as they moved, their hands and feet unfailingly finding purchase in the rock wall. Tyler counted ten, eleven, twelve more. The second Visitor reached the fissure's lip. It dug into the rock with its sharp, angular knees and pulled itself up, standing to full height in front of Felix Hill. Hill tried to speak, but the second Visitor turned away before he could get a word out. It watched as the rest of its group climbed up and out, the crowd of humans retreating as each seven-foot figure emerged to examine them with identically dark, lidless eyes.

Not that they looked the same, Tyler thought. Each Visitor's face was shaped differently, as if slightly pulled in one direction or another during a younger, more malleable part of its life. Each gesture they made was slow and measured. They ringed the fissure's edge, watching as the last members of their group emerged and stood to join them. When the thirteenth member got to its feet, every Visitor turned and faced the crowd. Tyler glanced at Anna, whose eyes were unreadable in the near dark. Bernie stood beside her, still gripping Roscoe's collar with both hands, though the dog had sat down and was watching quietly.

"Tyler," Felix said, "ask the Visitor why they're here."

Tyler shook his head. Felix was waving at him from across the fissure. "The first one, Tyler. The alpha member. Ask it why they've come to earth."

Tyler leaned back and looked the alpha Visitor in the eye. "I've met one of you before," Tyler said. "He was in the mountains. He had a ship." The figure stared back at him. It had the same closed, thin line for a mouth. Tyler tried to clear his mind in case it was trying to send him a telepathic message. Instead, he noticed an ambulance siren wailing on the highway east of town, still several miles away, sent from Silverton in reaction to the earthquake. Soon there would be fire trucks, highway patrol cars. News vans. The outer world would converge on Wormwood and they'd find these beings standing in the middle of Main Street. Tyler wondered if the Visitors understood what this would mean for them.

The alpha Visitor stepped away from the fissure. The others did the same. The crowd parted as the Visitors clustered together, thirteen pale, towering beings in the middle of the earthquake-torn small town. Tyler grabbed Anna's hand and pulled her after him, not wanting to miss a thing. The Visitors, followed by the crowd, walked a block south through the ruined beer garden. The garden's orange fence lay on its side. The canvas bartender tent still stood, but the temporary bandstand had collapsed and the amplifiers lay tipped forward, like drunks in the gutter, and the other audio equipment lay strewn across the ground, still plugged in and sparking. The Visitors closed their ranks, walking in two narrow lines as they passed the debris. The crowd did the same behind them, taking their eyes off the aliens for the first time since their arrival as drunk and sober citizens alike picked their way through the carnival wreckage in the dim orange streetlight.

Felix Hill joined Tyler and Anna as the Visitors continued down the street, discarded plastic cups crumpling under their wide, hooflike feet. The aliens avoided the fallen Ferris wheel and the hardware store's smashed façade. Bricks and broken concrete blocks lay scattered everywhere. The Ferris wheel's lights flickered on, surged blue, and went dark again. The wheel's frame was bent and twisted, especially the section that had collided with the hardware store. Several gondolas had broken away from the frame and lay on their sides. As they emerged from the three blocks of street carnival wreckage, a group of four men appeared ahead of the Visitors, armed with rifles and shotguns. Felix Hill swore, breathing heavily. One of the men lifted his rifle into the air and fired a single cracking shot.

"Stop walking."

The Visitors pulled up. Their hands remained at their sides and they watched the men openly, their expressions unchanged. "You're not just going to waltz through our town and take our children," the gunman said. "This is America. We have rules against that sort of thing."

Tyler rubbed his right temple, unable to believe he'd just heard something so stupid. Did these idiots actually think this was a hostile invasion? Thirteen unarmed aliens on foot?

"Guys—"

"Shut up, English teacher. This isn't time for a book report."

"I don't know. Maybe it is, Rick."

The crowd rustled as Merritt Jackson appeared on horseback. He sat upright in the saddle, one hand holding Sadie's reins, the other free at his side. His cowboy hat had turned black with dirt. "He rode a pale horse," Felix whispered in Tyler's ear, "and his name was Death." Tyler frowned and squeezed Anna's hand. She smiled dreamily back at him and raked her hair with her other hand, combing out a snarl with her fingers. The Visitors remained motionless, eyes fixed on the men with guns.

"You can't let these things just walk through town, Sheriff. You don't know what they're liable to do."

"I don't know, Dan. They seem peaceable enough to me."

"They're aliens. You don't know what they look like friendly, or what they look like ready to murder."

Merritt dropped his head for a second. He patted Sadie on the neck and looked up. "I guess, fellas, you're just going to have to trust me. You elected me to keep the peace, and I think this is the best way to do that."

"Hell, Merritt—"

"Now put down your goddamn guns, boys. You're not only drunk, you're making the town look bad."

The armed men glanced at one another. Merritt unbuttoned his holster with his thumb. One man laid down his shotgun, and the others followed. They stepped back from the guns. "Thank you," Merritt said, touching his hat. "Now, let's see where these folks are trying to go."

The Visitors turned right off Main Street and headed west. They remained in a tight group, striding down the middle of the road while the crowd followed a respectful twenty yards back, led by Sheriff Jackson. The Visitors appeared to ignore their surroundings, turning neither left nor right as they passed through the residential area and the cacophony of barking neighborhood dogs. The earthquake had felled a number of old trees and they lay across lawns and driveways, reclining as if to watch the crowd pass. "It's a parade," Anna said. "It's the Meteorite Days parade."

Felix Hill laughed. It was a short, barking laugh, and Tyler glanced at him, wondering if the W.V.S. leader was losing it. It was one thing to prophesize first contact, but it was another thing to actually live to see it realized.

"Stunning, absolutely stunning," Felix said, gesturing toward the fluid group of beings walking ahead of them. "This entire time I believed they had not yet arrived, but here they were, living beneath our feet. What were they doing? Studying us, gauging our readiness for contact? Sleeping? And the earthquake. It must have catalyzed them to action somehow. Perhaps the meteorite emitted some type of homing signal to call them forth? Amazing."

The Visitors passed the last row of houses and continued past a DEAD END sign at the end of the street. They covered the rocky, sagebrush-cluttered terrain with the same easy fluidity, avoiding the vegetation instinctively, their eyes fixed on the night sky. The crowd of humans following them had more difficulty, tripping and stumbling through the desert as they tried to keep up. Only a few people had flashlights, and their small, white beams zigzagged erratically across the ground like water bugs on the surface of a pond. Tyler let go of Anna's hand to keep his balance and a few seconds later turned to find his wife gone.

"Anna?"

"She drifted off into the crowd," Felix said. "She seems to be marching to the beat of her own drummer."

"Where do you think the Visitors are going?"

"I don't know," Felix said. "They appear headed for the mountains. I'm sorry, Tyler. The society should have taken your contact experiences more seriously. It was arrogant of me to assume I'd be the one to encounter them first."

"It's okay. I didn't take them seriously myself."

The Visitors halted in a clearing. Merritt Jackson turned around and signaled for the crowd to stop. People stumbled over one another, jostling for a view as they formed a long, strung-out line in the desert, and they hushed as the Visitors craned their heads backward and peered directly above the open terrain where there was nothing to see but the moon and the stars. Their thin, closed lips opened and a high, whistling sound rose from their mouths. The skin along Tyler's neck tingled as the sound grew louder, a cross between a howling wind and a funeral keen. The children in the crowd put their hands to their ears and began to cry. Behind them, the dogs in town howled in response and a coyote cried from the mountain range and then the entire night was filled with the Visitors' shrill song. Their pale forms shone with the moonlight, tall and unearthly as they sang, and Tyler felt his chest tighten. Clyde Ringston should have been here to see this. And Cody, who loved star charts and astronauts and anything else that had to do with space. Cody should have been here to see this and stand by Tyler's side while humanity first encountered life from across the void, but he wasn't, he'd been absconded with. His father could drink and his mother could knit all the scarves she wanted, but Cody was gone. He would not be found.

The Visitors stopped singing and the dogs and coyotes ceased their howling. A shadowy bulk had risen above the mountains and was flying toward them. The saucer. The ship.

"My god," Felix said. "It looks just like the pictures."

"I know."

"I expected they were fakes. Hoaxes perpetuated by the bored and fraudulent."

"They weren't. I mean, some of them weren't."

"It's beautiful."

The ship, still cloaked in darkness, hovered above the desert and slowly settled on the ground in front of the Visitors. It appeared larger than Tyler remembered, about forty feet tall and forty feet in length, but it still gave off that cold that settled into your clothing and seeped through the pores of your skin, as if it had just come from deep inside a cave. The crowd rubbed their forearms and hugged themselves against the chill as a round door opened on the ship, like a mouth. Dim, golden light shone through the doorway and Tyler could make out a ramp descending, a ramp indented with wide steps.

The Visitors began to stride across the sand to the landing ramp. The crowd held back, cowed by the ship's mass. A small moan from Felix Hill faded on the wind.

"They're not here to meet us," Tyler said. "They just want to go home."

"How can you be sure?"

"Just look at them. They're homesick."

The Visitors climbed up the landing ramp one by one. None of them turned back before ducking into the ship and disappearing into the golden light. None of them waved good-bye, or gave a gesture of intergalactic fellowship. The crowd sighed as the last Visitor climbed inside the ship and was lost to view. Tyler squinted. Wasn't that a small being, standing to the side and peering out at the crowd? Wasn't that his old friend with the ancient eyes? Tyler waved at the figure. His friend gave a small bow (at least it looked like a bow) and the landing ramp slid up and the ship's door closed, presenting the crowd once again with a dark, united front.

Felix turned to Tyler and loosened the knot on his tie. "Do you think they've been here a long time?"

"Too long," Tyler said, remembering the pulled taffy look of their limbs, their stretched faces. "They've been here so long earth changed them. Maybe our gravity, or radiation from the sun."

Sand billowed beneath the ship as it rose soundlessly from the ground and into the sky. The crowd murmured as the ship flew east, angled its bow slightly toward a dense cluster of stars, and disappeared into space. Tyler set his hand on Felix Hill's shoulder. "We're on our own, man. But that's alright."

THIRTY-THREE

As the first surreal reports came in, the FBI rolled into Wormwood and put the entire town under quarantine. They posted roadblocks on the main highway and every side road and the town found itself under siege, its population doubled by federal agents and sweating, heavily armed soldiers in riot gear. Anna expected them to burst into everybody's house with their alien delousing gear, or whatever it was they used for situations like this, but instead the G-men made the town come to them, turning Wormwood's high school into an interrogation center while they processed statements from every resident in town. The high school parking lot was turned into a helipad as helicopters landed and took off at all hours, shuttling specialists in and out of town, and the bars and restaurants were packed nightly with unfamiliar, solemn-faced men and women speaking in low, measured voices as they drank whiskey and ginger ale.

Taco Thunder was completely destroyed. When Anna and

Bernie went to pay their respects to the Diaz family they found the house empty, the front door locked, and the minivan missing from the garage. No one ever saw the family again. Months later, someone bought Taco Thunder's lot and opened a tourist trap called the Meteorite Café, complete with blown-up pictures of the meteorite, the meteorite crater, and Mr. Diaz sitting inside his shelter, wrapped up in his recliner as he stared out at nothing with the "The End Is Near" sign on his lap. Anna heard that Rosa, fed up with Wormwood once and for all, had quietly packed up the girls and driven off while everyone was distracted by the Visitors, and she also heard that the Diaz family had been hauled away by the government, interrogated, and relocated in style after agreeing never to speak in public again about Mr. Diaz and the events in question. No funeral, not even a memorial service, was held for Mr. Diaz.

The casino was kept open during the quarantine and Anna worked her usual shifts. The few customers they had sat at the bar, talking endlessly of the aliens, aliens, aliens, until Anna wanted to shove cotton in her ears and scream for them to just shut the fuck up already. Okay, Tyler had been right: Spacemen had been lurking around town. So what? It was over now, and she doubted the spacemen were coming back. They probably hadn't wanted to land on earth in the first place. As far as she was concerned, the world just needed to move on already.

On Labor Day, the third day of the quarantine, Anna was summoned to the high school to give her deposition regarding what the government—and the media—were calling the Wormwood Incident. Guards were posted at the front of school, why she had no idea, and a woman dressed as conservatively as an Amish matron led Anna down the first-floor hallway, cradling a clipboard and speaking quietly into her headset. Anna ran her hand along the locker doors to her left, trying to call up memories of high school and homecoming and the three cheer squads she'd captained, but all she could picture was the meteorite, dark and silent at the bottom of its crater, negating everything else.

The agent led Anna to the history room and left her with a tired, middle-aged man sitting behind the teacher's desk, a colorful map of medieval Europe pulled down behind his head. The man had ruffled gray hair, bloodshot blue-gray eyes, and drank coffee from a forty-four-ounce plastic gas station mug. An empty grease-stained pizza box lay flat on his desk like cardboard road kill.

"Hello, Anna. I'm Agent Fredrick. Please, sit down."

Anna nodded and sat down on the metal folding chair across from the agent. The room smelled like hazelnut coffee mixed with B.O.

"Anna, I'm sure you know by now we're interviewing everyone in town about last Friday evening. There's nothing to be nervous about; this is only a formality. We're not here to single out any one person. We just want to get to the bottom of this."

"You mean the aliens. You want to get to the bottom of the aliens."

"If you'd prefer to put it that way, yes. So, did you witness the aliens personally?"

"Yes."

"You were downtown, at the street carnival?"

"Yes."

"And you were there during the earthquake, also?"

"Yep. I made sure the Ferris wheel didn't crush a bunch of drunks. They kept staring at it like they were hypnotized."

"Really? I'll have someone look into that. Maybe we can arrange to have a medal presented."

"That's okay. I'm not in it for the fame."

Agent Fredrick smiled and took a drink from his coffee mug. Anna wondered if he'd managed to sleep for more than ten minutes in the last three days. Here they were, two insomniacs in a high school chemistry room, shooting the breeze.

"Had you been drinking, Mrs. Mayfield?"

"When?"

"Before the earthquake."

"I'd had a couple of beers. I'd say I was still pretty sober, though. Is that the government's theory? That everyone in town was so drunk they thought they saw aliens from outer space?"

"Not exactly. We've found significant amounts of lysergic acid diethylamide in the town water supply."

"LSD? You think the whole town was on acid?"

"It would explain the mass hallucination."

Anna shrugged. "What about pictures? People must have taken pictures."

"We have a few grainy cell phone images, but they're in-conclusive. They could represent anything."

"So you're going to just cover this up?"

"I'm not going to do anything," Agent Fredrick said, leaning back in his chair. "I'm just a humble servant of the people."

The interview went on for another hour before Anna was led to another room where a female doctor with cold hands gave her a complete physical. Anna cracked a joked about having an alien baby and the doctor just looked at her, frowned, and went through her notes a second time. When the exam was over, they gave Anna a bottle of water and let her go. It was dark, around nine o'clock. As Anna walked home from the high school she saw a line of SUVs pulling onto the highway east of town, their headlights turned north toward Silverton. A helicopter rose thumping into the night, headed east. The roadblocks were gone. The quarantine had been lifted.

At home, Tyler was already asleep in their room. He'd slept for most of last three days, bogged down as he tried to process the realization of his nerd dreams. Anna got into bed with him and lay there, uncomfortable, a tight knot growing in the small of her back. She remembered the meteorite fragment and pulled it out from under the mattress. The plastic crinkled as she removed the evidence bag and flung it into a corner of their room. She held the meteorite above her face, looking at it in the dark. She liked how heavy it was; it would make a good hand weight, like the kind you were supposed to carry when you speed walked. She could start her own line of meteorite-based exercise equipment. She'd make millions and they could all retire to the Cayman Islands to drink daiquiris and snorkel. They'd fly Roscoe over in a big doggy crate.

Tyler turned in his sleep. Anna watched him for a minute before setting the meteorite down on the floor beside their bed. She got up without turning on a light and slipped on a T-shirt and running shorts. She went downstairs and got a glass of orange juice from the kitchen. The first floor was quiet: Bernie had gone to bed and Roscoe was asleep on the couch in the living room. Anna got out a lined yellow note-pad and a blue ballpoint pen and sat down with them at the dining room table.

I'm sorry, Ty, but I don't think I can do this. I can't take this town. I can't take you. I can't take any of this.

Anna paused and took a drink. The orange juice clung to the back of her throat, which felt sore and swollen.

Do your remember when we first met? I don't mean that stupid football game when Sam Lindberg a.k.a. Mr. Steroids went over-board and threw me too far in the air. I mean the week after that. The first months after we met, the first year. We were in college and everything seemed so promising. The future wasn't all screwed up yet. We were still young, and not in the way old people think your late twenties is still young, but really young. We could stay up all night making love and still get through our classes the next day.

I miss that. I miss it like you miss your brother.

I suppose that's shallow. But here's a big surprise: I'm shallow. What do you expect from a former Miss Nebraska? I used to put petroleum jelly on my teeth to make them gleam under the lights. Petroleum jelly, Tyler. No one should have to do that. No one should want to do that. But I did, and I wanted to. There's something wrong with me. There's something seriously screwed up in my cogs and sprockets. When I read fashion magazines, I imagine what all the women look like naked. Not in a sexy way, though. I picture stretch marks, hairy moles, and those red bumps you get from shaving your bikini line. I picture little rolls of fat that appear when they sit up in bed and hunch over to paint their toes. I want to know they aren't as beautiful as they appear to be, and that's because I'm not as beautiful as I appear to be. I'm a fake. A big fat fake. I don't even know what I want to do with my life. I can't waitress forever. I'm already getting wrinkles under my eyes, just like my mother, and it'll be downhill from here. Before you know it, I'll be that ugly, drunk old lady at the bar, smoking too many cigarettes as her skin turns to leather, laughing too loud when men in polo shirts and golf tans tease her about dressing like a twenty-year-old.

When you suggested moving out here, I thought this might actually work. A new location, a new town, a whole new life where I could figure myself out once and for all. How wrong was I about that? All I've done since we moved here is have fucked-up dreams, see fucked-up shit, and work in a fucked-up place. I mean, when I saw those aliens climb out of that pit I started to feel happy, really really happy, because didn't this mean the world had to change now, had to realize that what we see isn't everything, that there's more to life than just surviving? For some reason that idea made me so happy it was like I started to drift outside myself and I felt it all, the whole universe, every molecule of it, and it was good and it all meant something.

But then the aliens left, didn't they? They didn't care about us. They only wanted to go home. They left us behind to be quarantined and covered up with government sand, and a few years from now Friday night is going to fade from our memories and in a hundred years it'll just be another myth in a desert filled with them. Soon all this trouble, all this crazy earthquake meteorite trouble, won't mean a thing.

Don't get me wrong, Ty. You've been great about it all. You've been a real trooper. You take my bitchiness and somehow change it into love, and that's pretty impressive. Not a lot of guys would have stuck with me like you have. I'm still glad you were there that day at Memorial Stadium, waiting to catch me. I could have done a lot worse. It's just that, look at my parents. They've lived together all these years and it's like they're a pair of old slippers and about as exciting. Do you really want us to be like that? Do you want to get old and drool all over yourself and shuffle around some nursing home? Do want to have kids and worry about losing them? Do you want to invest all this time in me and then one day, poof, an earthquake comes along and swallows me up?

You know, I don't think the world is actually going to end any-time soon. That's the scary part, actually. We're going to keep liv-ing and time will keep on ticking and when we finally punch out, life will go on without us, and maybe, okay, maybe that makes me a little jealous. Maybe I'm like that seven-year-old rich girl princess at a children's birthday party who doesn't want anyone to eat her cake except her. I told you I was shallow, didn't I?

You deserve someone better than me. You deserve a girl who bakes really good banana bread and gives backrubs and laughs at your stupid jokes and never teases you for squinting all the time like you're some kind of Chinese game-show host. So I'm going to take the Volvo and keep on driving. I don't think I'll go back to Ne-braska, though. You were right about leaving there. I think I'll keeping driving west past Lake Tahoe and Sacramento and visit San Francisco. From there, maybe I'll head north along the coast and see Oregon and Washington and then head into Vancouver for a while and talk with some Canadians.

I might even get snow tires put on and go all the way to Alaska. Hell. Why not? Life will swallow you and me and everyone else who tries to hold on to something and love it. That is what life does. That's its job.

I'm sorry,

Anna

Anna sat back and set her pen on the table. She shook her hand out and massaged the aching flesh between her fingers. She tore the pages out of the notebook and reread her letter slowly, as if someone else had written it. The paper felt dry and fragile in her hands. She tried it out, ripping a strip off the first page. She liked the sound the paper made as it tore, so she kept tearing, strip after strip, until the entire letter lay in the middle of the table like a yellow and blue paper haystack. Pleased with her work, Anna swept the pile off the table and dropped it into the kitchen wastebasket. She set her empty glass in the sink and headed upstairs.

The bedroom was dark, the only light coming from the orange street lamps out front. Anna avoided the sharp rock lying on the floor, slipped into bed, and curled on her side. Beside her, Tyler dreamt of a long, spiraling stairway that led to the cavernous center of the world, to an enormous pocket of open space. Within the space, the Wormwood meteorite hung in midair, pulsing like a heartbeat. Shadows drifted around the meteorite in slow, peaceful orbits, untroubled for the next ten thousand years of prosperity and strife.

Anna closed her eyes and fell asleep.

She didn't dream.